Death  in the Village

Phillip Strang

BOOKS BY PHILLIP STRANG

DCI Isaac Cook Series

MURDER IS A TRICKY BUSINESS
MURDER HOUSE
MURDER IS ONLY A NUMBER
MURDER IN LITTLE VENICE
MURDER IS THE ONLY OPTION
MURDER IN NOTTING HILL
MURDER IN ROOM 346
MURDER OF A SILENT MAN
MURDER WITHOUT REASON

DI Keith Tremayne Series

DEATH UNHOLY
DEATH AND THE ASSASSIN'S BLADE
DEATH AND THE LUCKY MAN
DEATH AT COOMBE FARM
DEATH BY A DEAD MAN'S HAND
DEATH IN THE VILLAGE

Steve Case Series

HOSTAGE OF ISLAM
THE HABERMAN VIRUS
PRELUDE TO WAR

Standalone Books

MALIKA'S REVENGE

Copyright Page

This work is registered with the UK Copyright
Service

ISBN: 9781718103078

Dedication

For Elli and Tais who both had the perseverance to
make me sit down and write.

Chapter 1

One minute, Gloria Wiggins was there in the main street making idle gossip, her passion as well as her hobby, and then the next, she was dead, a rope around her neck and hanging from a beam in the garage of her house.

There were some that said it was poetic justice, retribution for the malignancy that she had perpetuated for too long. And some still blamed her for the death of the previous vicar after she had stood up in the church one Sunday and denounced him.

The vicar, justifiably distraught, had left the church and headed out of the village on his motorcycle, only to slip on a patch of ice and go headfirst into a tree, cracking his helmet as well as his head.

Mrs Wiggins – no one remembered her husband, and believed him to be a figment of her imagination – saw it as the hand of God, and that her outburst was only the Lord talking to her to denounce the sinner. And now, the evil-mouthed woman was dead, and Stephanie Underwood, her next-door neighbour, along with virtually everyone in the village was not sorry to see her go.

Salisbury wasn't that far away, only twenty-two minutes if the traffic on the main road two miles away was flowing, forty-five if it wasn't, but Stephanie Underwood wasn't bothered either way. For the last twenty-eight years, she had not left the village, except for the occasional emergency: root canal surgery, a touch of gout, an irregular heartbeat, and shortness of breath.

Out there was a world of people and motor cars and exciting things to see and do, but not for her. She had completed her schooling, done well, five O levels, three A levels, and there were some, her parents included, who had thought she would go on to university, but never her. The village gave her what she wanted, and after her parents died, she had, at the age of nineteen, the cottage and their life insurance. Her days were routine: up at six in the morning, a walk around the area, and then back to her television. At ten in the evening, she would raise herself from her favourite chair, and go to bed. The only movement during those hours would be to feed herself and to commit to her ablutions. Now, the presence at her door of two people she did not want to see, and her favourite programme on the television as well.

'Detective Inspector Keith Tremayne, Sergeant Clare Yarwood, Salisbury Police, Homicide,' the man said. Stephanie saw a man in his fifties, not too fit, a belly that covered the upper part of his belt. Alongside him, a woman in her thirties, neatly dressed in a fitted jacket, a white blouse, and a skirt that was too short, knee-length.

'We understand that you found the body of Gloria Wiggins,' Tremayne said, momentarily talking to the back of the woman's head as she strained to look at the television.

It was Clare, Tremayne's sergeant for over four years, who moved into the house and turned off the television. It was one of her favourite programmes as well, but she'd watch it on replay later that evening, or whenever she had some spare time.

Stephanie Underwood, initially distracted by the police sergeant, focussed back to the question. 'Yes, I found her.'

'We need to sit down and take a statement from you,' Tremayne said. He could tell from how the woman dressed that fashion had passed her by and her clothes had a worn look about them. As if they had been purchased in a charity shop or retrieved from a clothing bin somewhere.

'If you must.'

'I'm afraid that this must be a distressing time for you,' Clare said, 'but we need to apprehend whoever committed this crime.'

'Distressing, I don't think so. I hated the woman, just an old busybody and a gossip.'

'Why such dislike, Miss Underwood?'

'She was always going on about God's damnation, and how those who did not give themselves wholeheartedly to God were condemned to burn in the fires of hell.'

'Were you one of those?' Tremayne said.

'I'm a regular church worshipper and a believer in the Lord, but Mrs Wiggins, she didn't hold with the modern world, and certainly not with television.'

'You do?'

'I've not left this village since I was a teenager, except a handful of times maybe. Not that I couldn't have succeeded out there, but I never wanted it, and besides, what do you have out there that I don't? Peace of mind, comfort, a stress-free life?'

The two police officers had to concede her point. A succession of murders, a health scare for Tremayne, an indeterminate love life for Clare, and a superintendent at Bemerton Road Police Station who wanted results, as well as Tremayne's retirement, had left both of them jaded and not in the best of spirits. However, a good murder always seemed to bring something to them, a focus away from the realities, and the village of Compton had all the ingredients for intrigue, as well as people who professed one thing but believed in another. And here, in the front room of a thatched cottage, was a woman who pretended to be normal, yet had rarely left the village in decades. It was ten minutes by car to the outside world, thirty to forty if someone was willing to walk across the fields, yet normality for Stephanie Underwood was a cottage with a television, her window to the world. She had all the makings of an eccentric, possibly a murderer, considering the woman hanging from a rope next door. Yet Stephanie Underwood was coherent and able to converse intelligently.

'Let's come back to when you discovered Gloria Wiggins,' Clare said. She was conscious of the woman looking at her skirt riding up her legs. She adjusted it and pulled the hem down. Stephanie Underwood clearly did not approve of legs and cleavage, or any attempt at enhancing the female form by the use of makeup and deodorant, her hair matted as if it was a bird's nest. Not one creature moved around the house, no dog, no cat, no fish in a tank, apart from a field mouse that scurried across the floor.

'She lived next door. We used to speak, even though we hated each other.'

'Why?'

'Why not? Just because I hated her doesn't mean I had to ignore her, does it?' It did to the two police officers, but it was not for them to comment.

'Do you make a habit of looking in the woman's garage?'

'Sometimes. And sometimes, she would be looking around here.'

'You've said you hated her, but it sounds as though you were friends.'

'You'd not understand.'

'Try us,' Clare said.

'The woman was frustrating, bigoted, a zealot who never had a good word to say about anybody or anything, but she was entertaining. I used to tease her relentlessly, but she never knew it. Not too bright was Gloria.'

'Whereas you are.'

'I was, still am. Sometimes when I'm not watching the television, I get out my laptop and surf the net, learn new things, visit new places.'

'Yet you've never been to any of them.'

'France once, a school excursion, but apart from that, no.'

'Coming back to Gloria Wiggins,' Tremayne said.

'I was over there looking around. One of my plates was missing out of the kitchen.'

'And you thought she could have taken it?'

'She was a kleptomaniac, not that she could help it, but she'd take anything that wasn't secured. She even once took a cross off the altar in the church, not that she intended to sell it.'

'What did she intend?'

'Nothing. It was just an affliction.'

'And your affliction?' Clare said.

5

'I've no interest in what happens beyond this village.'

'But you watch it on the television.'

'That's not the same as being there, is it?' It was to Clare.

'Gloria Wiggins, what happened when you found her?' Tremayne said.

'I looked in the house, it's always unlocked. I couldn't find anything of mine there, so I walked around the garden, looked in the garage. She was hanging there.'

'It's murder.'

'Plenty will be glad she's dead, not so sure that any would have wanted to kill her.'

Once free of the police officers, even escorting them as far as the front gate, Stephanie Underwood returned inside and switched on the television again, cursing them for interrupting her routine. She looked out of her window at the house next door. She could see the people in their coveralls and their gloves, as well as the masks they were wearing. Also others who were looking for fingerprints, knowing as Stephanie did that they would not find any.

Chapter 2

Tremayne and Clare walked through the village; a small river ran to one side of the narrow road, several small fish darting over the stones at the bottom, hiding in the reeds. A man stood in the water, fishing. He was dressed in neoprene waders, his net ready on the river bank. Tremayne thought he was ambitious, judging by the size of the net and the fish in the river.

'Not much of a feed,' Tremayne said by way of idle conversation.

'It's relaxation,' the man said, the casting of his line affected by the interruption.

'Police, have you got a moment?'

'Gloria Wiggins?'

'You knew her?'

'You never said who you are,' the fisherman said, putting his fishing rod to one side and returning to the riverbank.

'DCI Tremayne and Detective Sergeant Yarwood, Homicide.'

You're Tremayne, I take it,' looking at the older of the two.

'I am. What did you reckon of the woman?'

'She'll not be missed.'

'That's a bleak view of her. Most people feign sadness at the passing of another, especially if they've suffered a violent death.'

'The vicar who died. You've heard about him?'

'Does it have any relevance to the death of Gloria Wiggins?' Tremayne said.

'They're not biting, probably something to do with her,' the man said. 'Rupert Baxter is my name. The vicar was my younger brother.'

'What happened?'

'Our father tried to toughen him up, took him out running, enrolled him in the local football team, but it wasn't going to work. James eventually found God, and for many years his devotion suppressed his needs.'

'Gay?'

'Today's society may accept it, but it was illegal up until 1967. Before that, you could get two years in prison, but then you'd know that.'

'Before my time,' Clare said. 'Although we learnt about it, part of our training.'

'Your brother,' Tremayne said.

'It was 1998, so it wasn't against the law, although most people in this village didn't approve. James was the local vicar, doing a good job, but if his superiors had ever found out, he would have been defrocked, or whatever they do. Nowadays, it's not so much of an issue. Anyway, James had his eye on a farmer's son not far from here. Both of them were over the age of consent, but Gloria Wiggins caught sight of them holding hands once. James, he never did anything wrong, but we all need some fondness. The next Sunday, the woman is standing up in her pew denouncing James, a pawn of the devil, a sinner, a buggerer, a sodomite. Gloria Wiggins always had a colourful turn of phrase, especially when she was criticising someone, which was most of the time.'

'What happened to your brother?'

'James loved his church and tending to the needy. He knew that the woman's condemnation would get to the ear of the bishop, and it would be all over for him. He was a keen motorcyclist, surprising for someone who was only slight, but he was good. He even raced them when he was younger. He had a BMW motorcycle, a powerful machine. He took off, giving it plenty of stick, no doubt trying to get the pent-up frustration and anger out of him. He rounded a corner not far from here and slipped on some ice. Straight into a tree, head first. I never saw him, not when they peeled him off, but later on I identified him at the funeral parlour.'

'Gloria Wiggins?'

'She went around the village telling everyone it was God's retribution. No compassion from her, nor from Bert Blatchford and his wife, and some others in the village.'

'The same as her?' Clare said.

'The same. There are others in the village who were not too comfortable with James's issue, but he was a good man, and he could have done a lot for this village.'

'The current vicar?'

'He doesn't have the passion that James did.'

'And the farmer who had taken a shine to James?'

'He married a local girl, three kids now. Not that he ever goes to church.'

'And you?'

'I'm there every Sunday, more for James than the man upstairs.'

'When they bury Gloria Wiggins?'

'I don't think I could attend her funeral, although James would have said I am wrong. He saw the good in everyone, even when there was none. If you want my advice, check on who the woman maligned. It'll keep you busy for a few weeks just getting through them. Now, if you don't mind, I might just find my way down to the pub, have a drink, talk about the one that got away.'

'That'll not be the subject today,' Tremayne said.

'Don't I know it. It'll be Gloria Wiggins, and how we should drink a toast to her.'

'You won't.'

'Not me. She destroyed my brother, I can't forget that.'

'A motive for murder?'

'It is, but if you want to check, you'll find I was forty miles from here when she died. Cast-iron alibi.'

'We'll take a statement from you later. And we will check. Where can we find you?'

'At the pub. I'm the publican.'

***

The crime scene investigators were still busy when Tremayne and Clare arrived back at the dead woman's house. In the garage, she was still hanging. Around her, a group clad in coveralls, gloves and overshoes moved around. On one side, Jim Hughes, Salisbury's crime scene examiner, the person in charge of the assembled team. Young, still in his thirties, although closing in on forty rapidly, he was a man that both of the police officers respected.

'Another one, Tremayne,' Hughes said as he saw Tremayne and Clare arrive.

'As you say,' Tremayne said. 'What do we have?'

'Female, mid-fifties, no obvious ailments, and without further advice, I'd say in good general health.'

'The cause of death?'

'Strangulation by hanging.'

'Any noise?'

'Some, but it wouldn't have necessarily been enough to wake the neighbours.'

'Could it be a suicide?' Clare asked.

'Not this time. The woman was hauled up, the noose around her neck. The rope was tied off to a post in the far corner of the garage. This was premeditated as there are clear signs that someone had thought it through. She may have been unconscious when she was raised, or possibly semi-conscious. Pathology may be able to help you there, but I'd say she was not conscious. It's strange that people see these villages as havens of tranquillity, friendly neighbours, devoid of crime, when they're just the same as everywhere else.'

'The general verdict so far is that Gloria Wiggins was not popular,' Clare said.

'It's a motive, and whoever wanted her dead was not the sort of person who acted on the spur of the moment. Lifting the woman, and she's probably about hundred and sixty pounds, would have required some planning.'

'And someone strong,' Tremayne said. He was looking around the garage, having kitted up before entering, knowing full well that Hughes was pedantic about protecting the evidence.

'You'd think so, but there's a set of pulleys off to one side. We're checking, and it may be that whoever it

11

was had used the pulleys to lift her up and had then tied off the rope.'

'Someone not so strong, is that what you're saying?'

'It's a theory, although it would need someone with a degree of mechanical aptitude.'

'It's farming country,' Clare said.

'You're correct. If a tractor is stuck in the mud, no doubt both men and women would know how to use a winch and pulley. Even so, the pulley system could lift the woman, but then there's the tying off of the rope. Whoever it was, they took their time.'

'How long?'

'One hour, maybe less.'

'And why the garage? It's not the most pleasant of places,' Tremayne said. 'No sign of a car?'

'None that we can see. It was used more like a storage shed than anything else. The woman next door, any help?'

'She heard nothing, nosy though.'

'Practical?'

'She's a suspect, and she's educated, by her own admission. She's addicted to the television.'

'We've taken her finger and shoe prints. We found them outside on the garage door. So far, we've not been able to find evidence that she entered the garage.'

'And I was looking forward to a couple of quiet weeks,' Tremayne said as he and Clare walked away.

'Not you. This is what keeps you going, and don't deny it.'

'Yarwood, we'll need to do something about your attitude, too disrespectful of your superiors.'

Clare knew she was not. Tremayne was ageing, she could see it, and in the office at Bemerton Road

Police Station he showed every year of his life, plus a few more. In the office, he looked in his mid-sixties. In the village of Compton, ten years had come off, and he walked properly, no more shuffling along, no more rounded shoulders. He was in his element, and so was she.

Chapter 3

Tremayne had to agree that the local pub served good beer. He and Clare had walked the short distance from the dead woman's home to the pub, always the best place to get the feel of an area, the mood on the street. In one corner, an elderly couple sat. The man looked the fitter of the two; the woman had the countenance of someone who had just been told bad news, which, according to Rupert Baxter, the no-luck fisherman and jovial host of the Compton Arms, she had.

'Bert Blatchford and his wife,' Baxter said. He had poured a glass of red wine for Clare. The pub was warm, an open fire burning in one corner. On the walls of the cosy bar were horseshoes, antique farming implements, a couple of photos taken fifty years previously of two small boys and their parents standing outside the pub. The cars in the street Tremayne recognised from his youth when he had been first interested in cars: a Vauxhall Victor, a Ford Consul. At the time they had seemed to his young eyes to be the epitome of motoring excellence.

Nowadays, only the most avid collector of British cars would regard them as anything other than underpowered and antiquated. The sort of machines that had doomed the British car industry and allowed the Japanese to enter unhindered.

'That's me on the left,' Baxter said. 'The skinny kid to my right, that's James.'

'Did your family own the pub back then?' Tremayne said.

'Three generations. It was James that broke the mould. He liked the occasional drink, even as a vicar, but he had this revelation.'

'Revelation?' Clare said.

'Not that I understood it, but James came back one day from a walk. He was nineteen, mad on motorbikes even then, and he said a voice spoke to him.'

'What did you think?'

'I thought he'd gone a little crazy. James was always sensitive, and people, especially some of our contemporaries in the village, even some of the old-timers, used to give him a hard time on account of his being effeminate.'

'You've inferred that before, but riding motorcycles seems incongruous.'

'He was a contradiction, and he was an amateur cyclist before he got his licence. He took to motorcycles with no trouble. I could never get the hang of them. I rode one of his bikes, an old BSA 650 twin, and came off, broke both of my legs. On a motorbike, he was a macho man, off of it, he was just James. Anyway, he comes back, tells our parents and me, they're dead now, that he's going to follow the path of the Lord.'

'Did it upset you and your parents?'

'It did at the time, but James went off to study theology. A few years later, he's back here as our vicar. Those who had ridiculed him before showed him the respect he had always wanted.'

'And then Gloria Wiggins?'

'Yes.'

'Your relationship with her?'

'Civil. I hated her, she hated me.'

'That's how Stephanie Underwood described her relationship, but with them we got the impression of an underlying friendship coupled with an innate hatred,' Clare said.

'Stephanie's a queer bird, you know that,' Baxter said. He was on his second pint, so was Tremayne. Clare kept to the one glass.

Baxter left and went back to serving the other customers: a young couple who did not look to be local, a man who had come in on crutches, a couple of middle-aged women who both ordered gin and tonic. A burly man, taller than anyone else, stooped to get under the beam above the entrance to the two-hundred-year-old pub.

'There are some that say the place is haunted,' Bert Blatchford said.

'We've not introduced ourselves,' Tremayne said as he and Clare sat down next to the man and his wife.

'You're here to find out who murdered Gloria, aren't you?'

'Detective Chief Inspector Tremayne, Detective Sergeant Yarwood,' Tremayne said. Both of them produced their warrant cards and showed them. Bert took a cursory glance, his wife continued to look the other way.

'He did it,' Blatchford's wife said. Clare instinctively did not like her, although her husband, a ruddy-faced man, the sort of person who spent a lot of time outdoors, appeared approachable, almost friendly. Tremayne had told her, however, not to judge people on first impressions. She had learnt that lesson well. Her first great romance, a publican in Salisbury, had turned out to be a murderer, but time had moved on, painfully slowly for her until she had found someone else, a doctor this time. The man was treating her well, and she was enjoying his company, but once bitten, twice shy. They had been out a few times, including a romantic weekend in London where he had professed his love, but she hadn't, and it had put a dampener on their time away. He was looking for marriage, she knew that, so was she, but she wasn't sure if it was him or her that wouldn't allow her to commit. She had a career that she enjoyed, a man she could spend time with, but marriage meant divided commitments, although, as her mother reminded her all too often, she wasn't getting any younger, and in her thirties the biological clock was ticking. The inevitable lecture always came with 'when I was your age, you were already eight and doing well at school, and what a joy you were to your father and me. But now, what are you? A police sergeant traipsing around Salisbury with an old man when you could be up with us in Norfolk, running the hotel, ensuring your legacy, finding yourself a good man and settling down, giving me a few grandchildren.' Clare knew that she and her mother did not get along. Her father, a quieter person, said little, only to nod and shake his head at the right times when his wife was talking. Clare loved him dearly.

'Who did?' Clare said. She had moved round to where Blatchford's wife was looking. She could see a hard woman: her eyes dark, her complexion fair. Across her left cheek was a scar.

'Him at the bar, Rupert Baxter. He hated her.'

'We've been told the story about his brother,' Tremayne said.

'Not the truth,' Sheila Blatchford said, finally turning around to join the conversation. Clare moved back to her previous seat.

'What is the truth?'

'Rupert Baxter told you it was holding hands?'

Bert Blatchford showed his empty pint of beer to Baxter. 'You're paying if you want us to talk,' he said to Tremayne.

Tremayne could have said that a trip to Bemerton Road Police Station and the interview room would have made the man talk, but a few drinks in a warm pub often loosened the tongue more than a cold metal chair, an austere room and an electric heater in one corner. He shouted out across the bar. 'Make that two.'

'Three,' Sheila Blatchford said. Clare held her glass, placed the palm of her hand across the top of it. One person needed to be sober.

Baxter came over, placed the three pints on the table and left. No words were exchanged, other than a thank you from Tremayne.

'Coming back to what you said before, Mrs Baxter,' Tremayne said. He was on his third pint, his last for the evening. There was a time, not so long ago, when he would have drunk six, but that was before the health scare that put him in hospital, and before Jean, his former wife, had moved in with him. They were still discussing getting remarried, but neither seemed committed to the idea. The relationship was comfortable, and they complemented each other. Their life was not the mad passion of youth when they had first met; now it was calm and mature, and even Tremayne had to admit that a quiet night at home with Jean suited him fine, more so than the boozy nights when he, as a police officer, should have known better. Once he had been so drunk that the officers in a patrol car that had come by while he rested by the side of the road had put him in the passenger seat and driven him home, even put him to bed. Not that it avoided having to stand up before his superintendent the next day and receiving a verbal: 'if it happens again, you're suspended and out on your ear pending a disciplinary'.

'He told you they were holding hands?'

'Words to that effect.'

'He's lying. James Baxter and the other man were, I can't say the word.'

'The relationship was not benign?'

'I don't intend to sully what I know with coarse language. They were committing themselves to the devil, that's all I know.'

'Do you have proof, Mrs Blatchford?'

'Are you asking if I saw them?'

'Did you?'

'I know, so did Gloria, and so did my husband.'

'Mr Blatchford, did you have proof that James Baxter was involved in a homosexual relationship?'

'I trust the Lord.'

'That's not an answer.'

'Our consciences are clear, so was Gloria Wiggins', a good servant of the Lord.'

'A dead servant,' Clare said. 'Are you sorry that she's dead?'

'One of God's children, yes.'

'That's not an answer,' Clare reminded her.

19

'She was not a nice person, but she did not deserve to die.'

'And James Baxter did?'

'He had sinned, Gloria had not.'

'There are some that would say that speaking ill of your neighbour is not Christian.'

'We do not need lectures from those who do not believe,' Sheila Blatchford said. 'The good Lord condoned what Gloria did in that church, standing up and telling the congregation that the Reverend James Baxter was a sinner.'

'You were there?'

'We were.'

'Did you know what she was going to do?'

'No. But we would have agreed if she had come to us. We did not like her, any more than anyone else, but she was right. We can only commend her for that, and she is now with the angels.'

'One woman makes an accusation in the church, of which you have no proof, nobody does, yet you accept her word?'

'We did.'

'Why?'

'We don't need to answer.' Sheila Blatchford moved her seat and looked away. Clare could tell that she would say no more.

'My wife is upset over Gloria's death,' Bert Blatchford said.

'If you believe that Rupert Baxter killed her, then why are you in his pub?'

'If he hadn't, someone else would have.'

'Enough to kill her?'

A return to the conversation from the recalcitrant Mrs Blatchford. 'Our faith does not permit the killing of another,' she said.

'Nor does it allow the unsubstantiated accusation of a man without proof,' Clare said. 'A man who as an indirect result of that accusation killed himself in an accident.'

'The Lord giveth, the Lord taketh. James Baxter received his punishment.'

'He wasn't guilty of any more than a need to be loved. He didn't deserve to die.'

'Gloria Wiggins did not deserve to die, but Rupert Baxter killed her. Talk to him if you want the truth. He knew what his brother was.'

Chapter 4

As with any murder, the paperwork was not far behind. Tremayne missed the good old days before computers and key performance indicators. He could remember when the first computer had entered Bemerton Road Police Station; it had been heavy and clunky, and definitely not user-friendly. He remembered the superintendent, a young, enthusiastic, degree-educated man who had embraced it, not that Tremayne had liked him very much with his smug, holier-than-thou attitude. He was gone now, promoted up to London, and the current superintendent, still young, and always after Tremayne's retirement, was at least personable. Tremayne would admit to liking the man, but not to his face, and certainly not to anyone else.

That was how Tremayne operated. To his sergeant he was firm but caring, to his superintendent he was respectful but never condescending, to any criminal, murderer or otherwise, he was singular in his determination to apprehend them and to shut them up tight behind iron bars.

'These will revolutionise the police force,' the computer-loving superintendent had said all those years ago. 'No more offices filled with reams of paper, no more filing cabinets jammed full of cases.'

Fine words, Tremayne reflected as he sat in his office, two filing cabinets to one side, a laptop in front of him, and twenty feet from where he sat, an alcove with three printers. Their function, it seemed, was to pour out reams of paper.

Tremayne looked at his laptop, saw that he needed to enter the date, generate a case number. He knew he could manage, but it did not interest him. He closed the lid and went outside to talk to his sergeant, someone who did enjoy laptops and reports. He had tried, but she seemed to be at home with them, even admitting to being on Facebook, as well as reading book after book on the thing. He could only relate to a book if it came from a bookshop and it had a hard cover. There were some that saw him as a Luddite, he knew that, but it wasn't true. Progress was fine, so was technological advancement – if it assisted. But to him, paperwork at the start of any murder investigation, a mandatory requirement, was counterproductive. Out at Compton, there was a murderer, quite possibly a person who would not stop at one, and there were people to interview, people who may give a clue, not knowingly, but one comment leads somewhere else, and time was of the essence. So far, they had a woman hanging from a beam, a publican who blamed the woman for his brother's death, a next-door neighbour who disliked the woman, yet seemed to have maintained a cordial relationship with her, and a couple of less than charming people who hated her but still respected her.

There were close to one hundred and fifty people in the village. So far he and his sergeant had only spoken to four, and each of them had a motive.

'Yarwood, we've got a murder to solve,' Tremayne said. In the years he and his sergeant had been together, only once had he called her Clare. The time he had referred to her by her Christian name had been when her fiancé had died tragically, saving her life, ending his. It had been six months since his name had been mentioned by either of them. Tremayne hoped she had moved on, and the doctor she had been seeing had done her a world of good.

'Paperwork, it's important,' Clare said. She looked up at Tremayne, could see him champing at the bit. 'I'll do it later. Compton?'

'There are a few we need to talk to.'

***

The Reverend Jasper Tichborne was a man of moderate height, shorter than either Tremayne or Clare. They found him close to the church, dressed in a pair of old jeans and a grey jumper, and wearing heavy boots. Clare had to admit that he was not a bad-looking man, not exactly handsome, not ugly either. He stood from where he had been tending to his small garden when he saw the two of them arrive.

'Tragic,' Tichborne said.

'I thought you would be administering your pastoral duties at this time,' Tremayne said.

'We will be holding a service later today in her memory, not that many will come.'

'Why's that?'

'She was a good servant of the Lord, a devout parishioner, but…'

'But she was an unforgiving woman with a malicious tongue who nobody liked,' Clare said.

'It is not for me to talk of Mrs Wiggins in such a manner,' Tichborne said.

'True though?'

'It would be uncharitable, even unchristian, for me to agree with you.'

'We're police officers,' Tremayne said. 'We deal with the truth, not whether it's uncharitable or otherwise. Reverend Tichborne, if you believe she was not a good person, then say it. And if there are people in the village who would have harboured grudges sufficiently strong to have wished the woman dead, even murdered her, then tell us who. Nothing is to be gained by your reticence. If one woman has been killed, others may be at risk. We've met the Blatchfords. They seem to be tarred by the same brush as the dead woman.'

'Yes, Detective Inspector, she was all that you say. I had spoken to her on several occasions about loving thy neighbour, turning the other cheek, forgiveness, but I'm afraid it always fell on deaf ears. And yes, the Blatchfords are, as you say, tarred with the same brush.'

'Why?'

'Who knows? Some would say it was tempered by the good book. I can only tell you that Gloria Wiggins was a woman it was easy to hate, but murder?'

'Murder is usually committed by someone the victim was close to. Did she have such a person?'

The three moved away from where the reverend had been tending his garden and into the small rectory nearby. After cleaning his hands, the man of the cloth put on the kettle and made them each a cup of tea. Clare looked around where they were sitting, saw it to be lacking any feminine touches: no flowers in a vase, no attempts at arranging the furniture, no apple pie cooling on the windowsill, no patter of little feet. The rectory was functional and warm, nothing more.

'You live on your own?' Clare said, remembering full well that James Baxter had lived alone, and for a reason.

'My wife died five years ago. Since then, it's been the church and me.'

'I'm sorry if I've raised unpleasant memories.'

'No need to be. We had a good few years together before the Lord summoned her.'

'Coming back to Mrs Wiggins,' Tremayne said.

'Mr Wiggins, but no one has ever met him. She has lived in this village all her life, apart from a few years when she had lived in the north of England, something to do with her job.'

'Which was?'

'She always said it was secret, although who knows?'

'And the husband?'

'According to her, they had met in the north, got married, honeymooned in the Lake District, and then one day, he upped and left her. She was strong in telling everyone, don't know why. There was some in the village who reckoned he was better off, but whatever the truth, he's never been here.'

'It could have been him who killed her,' Clare said.

'It's a possibility,' the Reverend Tichborne said, 'Although I've no idea where he is. According to Mrs Wiggins, she hadn't heard from him for a long time, and

26

others in the village never even believed the story, only that she embellished the truth, and that she was a frustrated woman who caused trouble. Whatever, she was a person who could polarise the village.'

'The Blatchfords didn't like her, but they supported her, especially in the matter of James Baxter,' Tremayne said.

'And your view of James?' Clare asked.

'I take a more liberated view. I wasn't here, you realise. Gloria Wiggins was wrong in what she did, but as for his death, it was an accident, nothing more, and certainly nothing to do with divine intervention. The God that I believe in is benevolent and forgiving.'

'Mrs Wiggins' and the Blatchfords' God?'

'He has an edge to him that I do not believe exists. Rupert Baxter certainly hated the woman, not the only one, either.'

'And where do we find these people?'

'Just ask around. They tend to say their mind. No hesitancy to tell me when my sermons drone on.'

'And do they?' Clare said.

'Sometimes I tend to get carried away.'

***

Rupert Baxter was insistent with Tremayne that he had a pint of beer on the house.

'Later,' Tremayne said. 'Yarwood and I have got work to do. Two orange juices for now.'

Clare smiled when her senior's face grimaced as he drank the juice. The pub was warm, an excellent place to discuss the case, and there was no superintendent who wanted to be updated, no reports to be filled in.

'The husband?' Clare said.

'Find out what you can. If he exists, we'll need to establish his alibi, interview him if necessary.'

'Not many believe that he ever existed.'

'What they believe is not important. Find out what she was like before she left the area, talk to those who were her contemporaries, people she socialised with.'

'Stephanie Underwood is a few years younger.'

'Check on her while you're at it. This not leaving the village except for the rarest of occasions is weird. And what about her parents? How did they die? Stephanie was nineteen, and since then, any romances, indiscretions? Find the facts on her, and then dig up the dirt. See if there are any inconsistencies.'

'They'll all have skeletons,' Clare said.

'Then find them. Bring in help if you need it. Superintendent Moulton is not going to leave us for long on this one. No doubt the media will be down here at some time asking stupid questions. I'll deal with them if I have to.'

The burly man that Tremayne and Clare had seen on their previous visit to the pub came in the door. He moved over to where Baxter was serving drinks. He took hold of his pint and came and sat down in the chair alongside Clare. 'You need to talk to me,' he said. 'My name's Barry Woodcock.'

'Why is that?' Tremayne said.

'I'm the one that the Wiggins woman made the aspersions about.'

'The holding-hands friend of James Baxter?'

Clare could see that he was a farmer: the calloused hands, the overalls he wore, the smell of hay. Not that she found the smell unpleasant, as she had spent time around horses and farms in her youth.

'James was a good man, and regardless of what the woman said, we were just friends. I suppose for a time I was enamoured of the man. He was worldlier than me, better educated. He lent me books to read, and we'd discuss them for hours. He even introduced me to my wife. And as for what the Wiggins woman said, it was just lies. Maybe James, if he weren't a priest, would have wanted to take it further, but I never did. He was good to me, I was kind to him, but nothing ever happened. Not that I've got anything against those who do. I grew up here, so my views were clouded to the outside world, but James told me that people should live their lives as they see fit, as long as they don't harm anyone.'

'Mrs Wiggins did not believe in that concept.'

'I'm not sad to see her go, but she wasn't responsible for James's death. It was an accident, and he did like to ride fast. I went on the back of his motorbike once, scared me too.'

'Could you have killed her?' Clare asked.

'At the time of James's death, I was angry enough with her for what she had said, was saying, but no, I did not kill her.'

'We'll need to check your alibi.'

'At home with my wife and the children. It's not the best alibi, but it's the only one I can give you.'

Chapter 5

Finally, Tremayne could see that he had no option but to return to Bemerton Road Police Station and deal with the paperwork. He was pleased that he and Clare had travelled out to Compton, found a few more facts to add to the puzzle of the murder of Gloria Wiggins. Her body was now in Pathology and ready to be examined. Forensics had the rope used, as well as the pulleys that may or may not have hoisted her, although Barry Woodcock would have been strong enough to manage on his own.

Outside it was dark as Clare opened her laptop. A competent typist, she wanted to be out of the office by 10 p.m. and to enjoy a relatively early night. At home, her sole remaining cat would be waiting for her, as was a cold lasagne which she would probably heat in the microwave. It wasn't much of a life, she knew, compared to her friends back in Norfolk, who had all married young, had children, although two of them were already divorced. Feeling a little melancholy, she phoned Steve Warner, her paramour and a doctor at Salisbury Hospital, and a man who wanted commitment, something she could still not give.

'This weekend?' he said. He was still at work, the same as her. An emergency for him, a murder for her.

'I'll try. We're busy again.'

'So I've heard.'

'Where?'

'It was on the news, or maybe it was social media. Wherever it was, I know it's Compton and an old woman.'

'Not that old. She was only fifty-five.'

'Point taken. I've got to go,' Warner said. 'Someone's come in with acute appendicitis. We need to prepare him for surgery. Love you.'

'The weekend, I'll try,' Clare said as she put the phone down. She knew that she should have said 'love you' in return, but she couldn't. She enjoyed the man's company, even enjoyed sharing his bed, but love, she wasn't sure. If it was fondness, then she could give it. If it was spending time together, then fine, but the idea of a lifetime, she knew she wasn't ready.

Tremayne sat in his office looking at the screen. The instructions, self-explanatory, were there, the procedure to follow was clear enough, but he could not see the point. The reporting was fine when they had a culprit charged and locked up in the cells below; a confession, hopefully, irrefutable proof if not. With one finger of each hand, he commenced the process: name, date, crime, witnesses, and so on. He would give it two hours, and then he would go home to Jean. She'd be asleep by then, but he knew she would wake up for him, make him a cup of hot chocolate, listen to how his day had been, and if he was hungry, ensure that he had something healthy and nutritious; not necessarily what he really wanted, though. He smiled at the thought of her when they had been married, only not to see her for nearly thirty years after their divorce, while she had taken off and married another man, had a couple of children, been widowed. Now she was back with him. And what had he, Detective Inspector Tremayne, done? A few live-in girlfriends, a few one-night stands, but apart from that, a house in Wilton, three miles from Salisbury, nothing special in itself, and a police pension. He knew that Jean would never complain, but he felt regret that two people who should have spent their lives together, hadn't. Tremayne looked over at Clare, saw her busy with her report. He looked back at his and continued with his typing, slow and rhythmic, but with no melody. *One hour, no more,* he thought.

***

An uneasy atmosphere settled over Compton, a village that had existed since the time of Magna Carta in the thirteenth century. And now it was about to be torn asunder, according to Bert Blatchford as he sat, or slightly swayed, in his seat in the village pub. The man was drunk, a not uncommon occurrence. Rupert Baxter could only see a man he did not like, but then Blatchford did not have a straightforward manner about him. He had made a career out of narrow-mindedness and a modest income from farming: a few dozen pigs, a dozen cows that gave milk, and over a thousand free-range chickens that gave him eggs which were sold at a premium price in the area. Also, each Saturday, outside the front gate of his farmhouse, there would be a stall with his produce, as well as his wife's home-made jams.

Baxter had to admit that the vociferous Mrs Blatchford could make excellent jam.

'Mark my words,' Blatchford slurred, making sure that the other patrons heard what he had to say, even if they did not want to, 'Gloria Wiggins' death will be avenged. And you, Baxter, the brother of that man, are in the firing line. You and the others, you all watch out.'

'Bert, you've had enough. It's time to go home,' Baxter said. 'I'll give you a lift.'

'Not you. And let me tell you, I'll never come in here again, never. Do you hear me?'

'It's not the first time, is it?' Baxter said. 'What about the time I criticised you over your pigs getting out from your farm, and what about that bad egg I bought off you. One word against you and you're not coming back. But here you are, about to fall over, and you're repeating yourself.'

In the bar were eleven people, and most were looking in Blatchford's direction. Baxter moved over to Bert and helped him out of his seat. 'I'll take him home,' he said. 'Five minutes and I'll be back.'

'Don't you touch me,' Blatchford said, pulling away. 'Not after what your brother did.'

'He got himself killed, no thanks to you.'

'Him and Barry Woodcock, the two of them up there in that field, late at night, I saw them with my own two eyes.'

'Come on, Bert,' Baxter said. What the man was saying wasn't right, he knew that, but it still hurt to hear him say it. He wanted to hit him to shut him up, but he would not.

'I'm going and on my own.' With that Bert Blatchford walked out of the pub and headed the short distance to where he lived.

'Instincts of a homing pigeon, has Bert,' Baxter said. 'He'll find his way.' The others in the pub smiled, some gave a subdued laugh. Baxter poured himself another pint.

***

Tremayne slept peacefully. He had arrived home at 11 p.m. Later than he had expected, but he had persevered and had completed the preliminary reporting required. When he had walked out of the door at Bemerton Road, he knew that he would sleep well that night and that the next day he and his sergeant could start in earnest, interviewing the villagers, digging into where they weren't wanted, unveiling the hidden truths that people carry. At home, Jean had woken and had given him a hot drink and a decent meal before putting him to bed, making sure that the alarm would not go off early.

At 1.30 a.m. both Tremayne and Jean were woken by his phone ringing. Jean answered, hoping not to disturb her sleeping partner. 'He's asleep,' she said.

'Sorry, Jean,' Clare said. 'You'll have to wake him. I'll be there in ten minutes. There's been another one.'

Clare picked up Tremayne as she had said. It had taken twelve minutes, not ten as she had initially said. Not that it was long enough for Tremayne, who staggered out of his house and sat in Clare's car, dragging the seat belt across and buckling it.

'It's Bert Blatchford,' Clare said. 'Dead and in with the pigs.'

'Did you ever watch *Silence of the Lambs*,' Tremayne said.

'The scene where one of Lector's victims was fed to the pigs? Not for me. I prefer something gentler, *Mary*

Poppins. Anyway, I don't think he's been in with them for that long, just a few hours. His wife found the body, phoned us straight away. I've phoned Jim Hughes. He'll have his crime scene team down there as soon as possible. He was about as happy as you were with being woken up.'

'Yarwood, you need to get a life. You seem to be revelling in my misery and this murder. Blatchford, not one of life's most agreeable men. How did he die, by the way?'

'According to his wife, there's a big knife in his back. Drunk, according to her. It appears that his getting drunk on weeknights, then singing the Lord's praise on Sunday and asking for forgiveness, is not an uncommon experience.'

'I can't deny that he's got his priorities right,' Tremayne said. 'There was a time before you and Jean ganged up on me when I could have a drink of a night.'

'And end up in Salisbury Hospital. The next time, Superintendent Moulton will have you out on your ear. Plenty of time for drinking then.'

The drive took twenty-three minutes, a better than average time for the trip out to Compton. At Blatchford's farm, a group of onlookers had gathered. There was a cold chill as they got out of their car, Tremayne's and Clare's breaths visible as they exhaled. Crime scene tape was tied off around the pigsty.

Tremayne walked over and looked in. The pigs were not there. 'I moved them,' Sheila Blatchford said.

'What can you tell us?' Tremayne asked. It was clear that the pigs had walked around and over Blatchford, but there was no sign of additional damage to the body, although if he had been killed there, there would be very little for the CSIs to find.

'Hughes and his team will be here in five minutes,' Clare said.

Sheila Blatchford appeared to be suffering delayed shock. She was still dressed in a dressing gown, and was pacing around nervously. Clare took hold of her arm to escort her back inside the farmhouse. 'It's him,' she said, pointing over to Rupert Baxter. She moved forward, holding a piece of wood. Clare grabbed her before she could go too far, and with both her arms wrapped around the woman took her inside.

Tremayne picked up his phone, called for a doctor; a sedative was needed. Baxter, initially standing nearby, retreated back to his pub; Tremayne watched him go. The man had not shown himself to be a great fisherman, although as a murderer he may have been more successful, and he had the strongest motive. Tremayne was not convinced, though. James Baxter had died a long time ago. Why wait until now to kill those who had approved of his death? And if Sheila Blatchford was still alive, would she be next?

The tranquil village, Tremayne knew from experience, had more intrigue, more secrets hidden in dark recesses, more reasons for people to die. He hoped that Bert Blatchford would be the last, but he knew that he probably was not.

Inside the farmhouse, Clare tended to Mrs Blatchford. The woman was still agitated, fluctuating between anger for the man she believed had killed her husband and sorrow for Bert.

Outside, the crime scene team had arrived, an ambulance not far behind. There would be questions later on as to why the ambulance with its medic had taken so long, but for now, the body took precedence.

'Why can't you get these to happen during civilised hours?' Jim Hughes said. Tremayne knew that Hughes' comments were not made with malice. He, along with everyone else at Bemerton Road Police Station, knew that irregular hours came with the job.

The CSIs kitted up, as did the medic. It was clear the man was dead, so no need for the medic who had come late to jump over the fence and rush to aid him where he was lying, his face covered by the mud and the excrement of the pigs. Tremayne donned the protective gear: coveralls, gloves, overshoes, and a mask. The smell was not pleasant, even from ten feet. It was going to be worse close up.

'Was he killed in there?' Tremayne said.

'If he was, there's bound to be plenty of footprints, although the pigs have probably destroyed them, let alone dirty clothes that the murderer would have been wearing. Find someone who's been doing some late-night washing, and you'll have your murderer. Although it appears he was murdered outside and pushed through the gate to the pigs.'

Hughes knelt down next to the body, another CSI taking photos, the flash lighting the area. A floodlight was being set up outside, another CSI running the power cord over to the farmhouse. Two CSIs were following the route from the farmhouse to the pub looking for clues, realising that the onlookers had sullied the area at the farm and the road close by. Tremayne was curious as to whether that was an intentional ploy or circumstantial.

'Knife wound to the back, deep enough to kill him, and then face down with the pigs, holding his face in the mud,' Hughes said. 'The back's not the best place. In front and into the heart would have been better. I'll assume the person wasn't proficient at their chosen task.'

'What about the pigs?'

'Good for bacon, not reliable as witnesses.'

Tremayne knew that humour, even at the worst murder scenes, was one of the ways that those there in the aftermath managed to stay rational and detached. Hughes could do it, so could he, but Clare was likely to get emotional. Tremayne knew that in time she'd get over it.

Inside the farmhouse, the widowed woman was sitting down, her two hands clasping a mug of hot tea. 'Why?' she said.

'That's why we're here. First Gloria Wiggins, now your husband. Is there anyone who hated them that much that they would kill them?' Clare said. She was also holding a mug, an attempt to empathise with the woman.

'Rupert Baxter. He hated Mrs Wiggins. He hated Bert and me.'

'Apart from him?'

'They all hate us, even the Reverend Tichborne.'

'Why would he hate you?'

'We never liked him nor his wife.'

'She died five years ago,' Clare said.

'She was always preaching about loving thy neighbour, even more than he did. Gloria Wiggins couldn't stand her, told her to her face, even hit her once.'

'When was that?'

'Nine, ten years ago. I can't remember exactly. The reverend's wife, a tall, skinny woman, head and shoulders above her husband, was berating Mrs Wiggins for criticising the previous vicar and his brother, saying that they were both as bad as each other.'

'Is Rupert gay?'

'Not him, but that was the woman. She didn't care much for the truth. She had a go at us once, thought

38

we spent too much time with animals, and she sure hated pigs, thought they were unclean, and we did not devote enough time to the Lord.'

'We were under the impression that you and your husband were as devout as her.'

'We are, or we were, but now Bert's dead and I'm on my own.'

'Family?'

'Bert wasn't much for children, and I couldn't have them anyway. The doctor said it was something genetic. Anyway, we got along, Bert and me. He wasn't much of a provider, but we never went anywhere, only up to the pub, sometimes into Salisbury. I used to like having a meal there when we went, a walk around the cathedral, tallest spire in England, did you know that?'

'Is it?' Clare thought feigning ignorance of the fact was probably the best approach, although how could she not know. Every tourist leaflet in the city pronounced the fact.

Tremayne knocked on the door and entered. 'The doctor is here. Is there anyone who can come and stay with you?'

'I don't need anyone. I'll miss him, but there'll not be a lot of grieving. And besides, the animals still need looking after, and then there are the chickens and the eggs to collect. I'll not have time to feel sorry for myself, and as for the sedative, I don't need it.'

Sheila Blatchford picked herself up from her chair, changed into her work clothes – heavy boots, a pair of men's overalls, a thick jumper, and a heavy jacket – and left the house by the back door. Tremayne and Clare watched her as she walked past the cows and the chickens, before leaning over to talk to the pigs. Neither of the police officers was sure whether she was admonishing them for walking over her dying husband, or whether she was thanking them.

'She's a suspect,' Tremayne said.

'She's a hater, that one. She could have killed Gloria Wiggins.'

'Her husband could have as well. It's not the end of the murders unless we find the culprit.'

'In this village? And what about Rupert Baxter? If he's killed two, he could still kill one more.'

'Too obvious,' Tremayne said.

Chapter 6

Gloria Wiggins had died a violent death; a full autopsy
was required. She was on the pathologist's table, a white
cloth covering her. Tremayne was present. Jim Hughes
and his crime scene team had not found much more that
was of value. It had been confirmed that Stephanie
Underwood, the next-door neighbour, had not been in
the garage, her prints only on the right-hand door of the
garage. It was old, and it still had its two wooden doors,
neither of which fitted well, as both had distorted with
age. There was a set of footprints on the driveway and in
the garage. The rope and the pulley had been placed in
position before the woman's death, no fingerprints on
either. And the killer had premeditated the woman's
death, which led to the possible conclusion that the death
had not been as a result of hatred, but as a result of a
disturbed mind. Tremayne was aware that some in the
village might qualify on that count, but unless a full audit
was conducted, then the latter possibility would be hard
to prove. And Bert Blatchford's death did not have the

characteristics of being premeditated; more spontaneous, with a quick thrust of a knife, at least a nine-inch blade, very sharp and serrated, and then a shove through the gate to where the pigs had been.

The CSIs had found evidence of someone else in the vicinity of the farm at the time, but no witnesses and no clues other than someone who would have had dirty clothes and shoes afterwards.

'Are you going to stay?' Stuart Collins, the forensic pathologist, said. Clare knew that the man did not appreciate being watched as he worked, not that Tremayne cared.

'Tell me about her death, and I'll leave you in peace,' Tremayne said. Out there in Compton was where the action was, where a murderer lurked in plain view, no doubt acting with all the innocence of committing a justifiable act, possibly a righteous act. Whoever it was, sane or otherwise, had serious psychological issues, Tremayne knew that.

'Preliminary observations indicate that the woman was conscious,' Collins said. 'We'll conduct analysis for signs of drugs. With the person soon becoming unconscious on being lifted off the ground, the full weight of the suspended part of the body fell against the rope, creating enough pressure to restrict air flow through the trachea. She would have lasted no more than a few minutes. Body temperature at the time of investigation by the CSIs indicates that she had been dead for five hours. A full autopsy will be conducted, the report forwarded to you in due course.'

'Thanks. That's all we need,' Tremayne said.

'I understand there is another one on its way,' Collins said. 'I hope you're not going to make a habit of this.'

'Visiting you or sending bodies?'
'Both.'
'I can't guarantee the second.'

***

Clare realised that the weekend date with the doctor wasn't going to happen. She phoned him to let him know that a murder investigation took precedence over her personal life, not sure if it was the end of the romance or an interlude – not sure which she preferred. Her mother would have said she was foolish, rejecting a doctor, an educated man, for a grizzled and seedy old police officer, but Clare would never agree on that analysis of Detective Inspector Keith Tremayne. To her, he was her boss, her mentor, her friend, although neither would admit to the fondness each felt for the other. It was only Jean, Tremayne's partner, who would mention it, invariably over a glass of wine, embarrassing them both profoundly, but then, that was why she did it. She was as fond of Clare as was Tremayne, having had two sons with another man, never a daughter. And to her, Clare was fulfilling that function, so much so that often she and Clare would meet up for a meal and a good chat.

In the village of Compton, an uneasy truce. In one corner of the pub, Rupert Baxter, the genial host: dispensing witticisms, discussing the weather, the upcoming harvest, the price of livestock. In the other, Sheila Blatchford, a glass of sherry in her hand. With her sat two other women, one man. The interaction between the man that she had accused and her was guarded and tense, but it hadn't prevented her giving her order, him bringing it to her table.

Tremayne sat to one side, observing. For the duration of the investigation, the Compton Arms would be his local, the best place to see all, hear all, and most importantly, observe all. And what had he seen? A woman who believed Rupert Baxter had murdered her husband, yet could talk to him, albeit without any sign of pleasure. To Tremayne, it didn't make sense, none of it did. Bert Blatchford was lined up for an autopsy with Stuart Collins, and the village acted as if nothing had happened.

Barry Woodcock walked into the bar, acknowledging Tremayne as he passed, a nod of the head. He ordered a pint, exchanged a few words with Baxter, and then headed over to Sheila Blatchford, offering his condolences at the tragic loss of her husband, and what a good man he had been, and how difficult it must be for her. The village was incestuous, definitely in its behaviour, possibly in its history. The Baxters could count three generations in Compton, the Blatchfords four, and the Woodcocks appeared to have lived in the village for over two centuries, probably longer. Clare had researched it for Tremayne and had passed over the details to his phone, one of the rare occasions when he used it. His sergeant was crazy for the thing, always talking to someone or another, but he kept it simple. A phone call when it was necessary, a received message when it was vital, a vibrating tone when he was in a meeting or interviewing someone.

Tremayne could see that Baxter was not talking to anyone, not serving either. He got up from his seat where he had been able to observe everything and moved to a stool round the other side of the bar where the beers were pulled.

'Another beer?' Baxter said.

'Just the one. I'm driving,' Tremayne said.

With two beers on the bar counter, one for Tremayne, one for Baxter, a brief 'cheers' and a clinking of the glasses, Tremayne spoke. 'I don't get it.'

'What don't you get?'

'Two people are murdered. You accuse Gloria Wiggins of causing your brother's death, along with the Blatchfords. Sheila Blatchford calls you a murderer, and here you all are acting as if nothing has happened.'

'We're a tight-knit family, that's all. We can hate, but we cannot ignore. And besides, we're used to helping each other.'

'It still doesn't make sense. Barry Woodcock, what about him?'

'James liked him, but you know that.'

'I do, but now he's talking to Sheila Blatchford and three others. Who are they?'

'The woman sitting down, looks as though her cat's been run over, that's Margaret Wilmot, dead for ten years some would say.'

'She's a miserable looking woman, I'll grant you that, but why the ten years.'

'She suffered a heart attack back then, her heart stopped, but somehow after a few minutes, then managed to get it beating again. There are some that reckon she never came back, and what you're looking at is a phantom.'

'A ghost?'

'It's nonsense, but she lacks any charm. The only reason Sheila Blatchford tolerates her is that they're united in their hatred of Tichborne.'

'He's an enlightened man,' Tremayne said.

'Not to them. Those two are all for fire and brimstone, strictly Old Testament, stone the sinners, raze the land of the Canaanites.'

'The other two?'

'The man sitting to the other side of Sheila, looks as if someone pushed his face in?'

'Your description, not mine,' Tremayne said. He had downed his pint, Baxter gave him one more.

'Hamish Foster. Scottish mother, English father. He had a nasty accident with a tractor when he was young. It rolled, smashed him up really bad. He still walks with a limp, and he had to have facial reconstruction. It's not that noticeable now, but it was bad once. We used to call him names when we were young, not very charitable I know, but that's what children do. Apart from that, he's not a bad man, certainly nothing like the others sitting there. The other woman, knitted top, flowery skirt, that's Foster's wife, Desdemona. Her parents watched a production of Shakespeare once, Othello. Supposedly she was conceived that night. It's her story, and she tells it well. Very pleasant if you get to know her, but she's susceptible to lost causes, stupid people. That's why she's talking to Sheila.'

'Anything else?'

'Just one thing. Sheila's my sister.'

'We checked. She's not a Baxter,' Tremayne said.

'Not on any records. It's bound to come out sooner or later, these things always do. My father, he was a man about town, or should I say, the village. Sheila's mother was on her own; it was before Sheila was born, and the man her mother had been married to had died. It wasn't so easy back then to find another man to take on a ready-made family, two sons already. A good-looking woman according to my father, and one night they got together. After that, it became a regular thing for a few years. Sheila was born, and her mother's husband was put on the birth certificate.'

'But he was dead.'

'No one was checking, and money exchanged hands. After that, the romance dimmed, but my father helped out financially when he could.'

'Does Sheila know?'

'She does. I've told you just in case there are DNA checks later on. I trust you not to reveal it unless you have to. Most people in the village probably know the story, but there are a few who don't.'

'I can't guarantee it. I'll have to tell Yarwood.'

'Another pint?'

'Not now. It's time to go. Jean will have a meal on the table when I get home. Cold probably, but she'll heat it up for me.'

'Lucky you.'

'You're not married?'

'I was, but it didn't work out. We had a son, although I haven't seen him for a long time. He may even be married with a family. I wouldn't mind making peace with him and his mother, meeting them sometimes.'

Chapter 7

There had been few in the village of Compton who saw Gloria Wiggins as anything other than dislikeable, and most believed that the Mrs in front of her name was an affectation on her part, an attempt to avoid the label of spinster of this parish. It was Clare who found it was not. She burst into Tremayne's office with the news, a welcome interruption from the paperwork that he had to deal with.

'Gloria Wiggins was married in London,' Clare said.

'Mr Wiggins?'

'He's alive and well and living about a one-hour drive from here.'

'You're driving,' Tremayne said, although to Clare that was not unusual. She always drove when it was the two of them, a chance for him to take a rest and to check the punter's guide, to find out which horse was going to win at the races that weekend, which one was going to lose. Clare thought that mug punter was more appropriate, as did most of those who knew Tremayne, but regardless, he would be weighing up whether the track was heavy, or if the horse had a good record of wins, the odds were in its favour, which way the wind was blowing. Even what star sign it was, at least that was what Clare assumed he took into account as well. One thing she knew, he had a lousy record when it came to picking the winning horse. When she and Jean, Tremayne's partner, got together, it often brought a few laughs to their conversation, especially when Jean recounted how she picked a horse on whether she liked its look, and how her record of wins was better than Tremayne's.

Cuthbert Wiggins, an old-fashioned first name for a man in his fifties, did not look the sort of person that Gloria would have married. A bank manager, he was a quiet man with a soft voice, the type of person who would get lost in a crowd of two. According to those in the village that had known Gloria, she was a forceful woman, loud of voice, always pushing in, monopolising any conversation.

'We were married for three months,' Cuthbert said. He was a small man and showed the signs of too many good meals and not enough exercise. He wore a navy suit with a white shirt and a striped tie. 'I was sorry when she left me,' he said.

'We need the full story. It may help us with our enquiries,' Tremayne said.

'I don't see how. She was an opinionated woman, and no doubt someone was offended. I was a junior in the bank back then, and Gloria and I were working at the same branch. I fancied her from the first time that I saw her, and soon, I think she must have asked me out, we were dating. After six months or so, I asked her to marry me, and she said yes.'

'Gloria always said that her job was secret.'

'Working in a bank? I don't think so. But then Gloria was ashamed of her job, of me eventually.'

'Murder's not a pleasant subject, but you, Mr Wiggins, don't seem concerned that she met a violent death,' Clare said.

'We parted a long time ago. It was acrimonious, at least from her side. I had a good nest egg as my parents had died young and left me financially sound. Gloria, she reckoned that six months of courting and then three months of marriage entitled her to half of the assets, went out of her way to secure them.'

'Lawyers pleading her case?' Tremayne said.

'You should have seen her. Obsequiously agreeable, and pretty as a picture. Not the battleaxe I had to confront every night after the first couple of weeks of marriage. I can remember her from back then, and then she won her case, took thirty per cent of my cash plus the house we had been living in. I was left out on a limb for a while, and with a bitter taste in my mouth. As far as I'm concerned, I'm not sad that she's gone. You probably think that I'm a right bastard, but I'm not. I'm just a man who loved the woman, and then she treated me like that.'

'Did she marry you for your money?' Clare said.

'I like to think that it was love, but yes, it was for the money. Gloria, if you have not already deduced it, was an unpleasant woman of few redeeming features.'

'She was not well-liked,' Tremayne said.

'I did not kill her, before you ask.'

'Why? Should we?'

'I read somewhere that statistically the nearest and dearest are the most likely candidates.'

'They are, but, as you say, it's been a long time. How long in your case?'

'The last time I saw her was that day at the courts when she almost jumped for joy when the verdict came through. I could have killed her that day, but not now. Eventually, I found myself another woman, and we've been married ever since, two children now.'

'Hatred lingers for a long time. You could have driven down to Compton and strung the woman up,' Clare said. She had to admit that she liked the lyrical manner of Wiggins' conversation. He was not an impressive man to look at, but he had an endearing personality, a wit that was subtle and constrained.

'I passed the hatred stage a long time ago. Life's good for me now, has been for many years. I didn't need that vexatious woman to disturb it.'

'We need to ask where you were on the day of her death,' Clare said.

'Either at work or at home with my wife. I'm not a traveller, never have been, although I'm partial to the occasional beer, so possibly the pub as well. Somewhere between the three is the best I can give you, and you'll find no gaps of more than an hour between any of them, not long enough to drive down to where Gloria lived and to kill her.'

'You knew where she lived?'

'We called in briefly the one time at her cottage, although no one else saw us in the village. It was no more than five minutes, and I never went in. All I could see were the paisley curtains, a depressing little cottage in a village that wouldn't win any prizes as England's loveliest.'

Tremayne and Clare would have to agree with Wiggins on that. The villages in the Salisbury area were invariably old and charming with their thatched cottages, their history, but Compton had changed since the last war, and most of the buildings were drab red brick with tiled roofs, not one having anything more than functionality. Certainly, that had been the case with Gloria Wiggins' thirties-era cottage. An unimpressive structure of three bedrooms, one bathroom, a front room reserved for guests who never came, a kitchen replete with a wood-burning stove, and an old refrigerator which continuously hummed.

With little more to be gained, the two police officers made their way back to Salisbury and to Bemerton Road Police Station.

'Nothing to say?' Clare said as they drove along, her in the driving seat.

'It's unlikely he murdered the woman, but we'll check out his alibi.'

'I'll get his local police station involved. And besides, Cuthbert Wiggins is a small man, Gloria was taller than him, no doubt stronger. He could have used the pulleys, but he would have had to get into the cottage, subdue her, and then drag her outside.'

'No sign of disturbance in the cottage which means she was either in that garage voluntarily, or someone had drugged her first.'

'Pathology found no sedatives or narcotics in her system.'

'We've still got the death of Bert Blatchford,' Tremayne said. He was leaning back as if in deep thought, although Clare could see that he was close to taking a nap for a while, a not uncommon occurrence. Age was creeping up on him, Clare could see that only too clearly, but she had been saying that for a few years, so had Superintendent Moulton, who was still after his retirement. Key performance indicators, the man would say, and it was probably true. Tremayne was the most experienced detective inspector at the station, yet he didn't have the obligatory degree, nor the adherence to police regulations that was required. He still believed in the no longer politically correct solution of 'give the villain a swift kick up the rear-end' instead of counselling him or her.

Clare had to admit the swift kick had prevented one or two that Tremayne had dealt with from getting into further trouble, and there were some in Salisbury who always welcomed him when he saw them: 'Remember when you beat some sense into me' or words to that effect. One was now the priest at a church in the city, another was on the city council, another was doing five years for robbery. Tremayne would admit that it didn't always work, but his success rate was better than the counselling. Clare, degree-educated, and a lot younger, was torn between the two approaches. Her phone rang.

'This weekend?' It was the good doctor checking to see if his and Clare's romantic interlude was on.

'He's keen,' Tremayne joked, not that Clare appreciated his comment.

'Not sure,' Clare said to Warner. 'We've got two murders and no suspects.'

'Then it's not, is it?' Warner said. Clare thought his answer condescending. She pulled a face at the phone, knowing that he could not see her.

'I'll try for the weekend after,' Clare said.

Back at the police station, a good hour to update the paperwork. Clare was soon into it, finished in twenty minutes, Tremayne took the full hour plus some more. After that, outside for Tremayne to smoke his obligatory cigarette, and then back to Compton. It was late in the afternoon, not that Clare minded. Her cat would be waiting for her back at her small place in Stratford sub

Castle regardless of what time she arrived home, and she knew her neighbours would feed it for her.

Compton looked even drearier as the two police officers entered the village. It had started to rain heavily, and the two of them made a dash for the warmth of the Compton Arms. Inside, Tremayne ordered a pint of beer, Clare kept to her usual glass of wine.

'Steak and kidney pie?' Rupert Baxter said.

'Fine by me,' Tremayne replied.

'Make it two,' Clare said.

In one corner of the pub sat Sheila Blatchford, her fire and brimstone comrades near to her. She had gained one more.

'Gladys Upminster,' Baxter said, noticing Tremayne looking her way. 'She's lived here all her life, not sure if she's ever left, other than for her Saturday trips into Salisbury for shopping.'

'Married?'

'Local farmer, Eustace. He's a good sort, always willing to pass the time of day, as long as you're interested in crop rotation, the price of sheep at the local market, the inclement weather not being good for farming.'

'A bore?'

'He is that, but he's not into Sheila Blatchford and her cronies. I like Eustace, so I talk about what interests him, and then he's fine.'

'A drinker?'

'That's him over there,' Baxter said, nodding his head in the direction of a man sitting on his own, a pint in his hand, a ruddy complexion, an old hat that had seen better days.

'Bring my meal over there,' Tremayne said.

Chapter 8

'Mr Upminster, if you could spare a few minutes,' Tremayne said as he sat down across from the man, his back to the man's wife who was intently listening to Sheila Blatchford.

'If you like,' the gruff reply. 'I was expecting to see you before now,' Eustace Upminster said.

'Why?'

'Motive, that's why.'

'What do you mean?'

'Plenty hated that woman, and a few of us weren't too keen on Bert Blatchford. The only good that I can see of either of them is as fertiliser.'

'Rupert Baxter said you were a man who only spoke about farming.'

'Baxter's right, but what else is there? You've seen those sitting behind you, my wife included.'

'I've seen them.'

'That Sheila Blatchford, a nasty piece of work, even worse than her dead husband.'

'What about them?'

'She draws the fools to her like a honeypot does to the bee.'

'Your wife?'

'A good woman when we were younger, but our son, he died in a car accident. It was a few years back, but she can't forget, forever looking for ways to atone for her sins, looking for forgiveness.'

'Forgiveness?'

'Our son was a tearaway and argumentative. I had hoped he'd grow out of it, but he was twenty-eight, and still going around as if he was in his teens. He was at home, nursing a sore head. Gladys was there berating him, and I was outside feeding the cattle, checking around the place. Our son storms out of the place, gets into his car and takes off at his normal speed. Anyway, five minutes later, he swings out in front of a bus heading into Salisbury, and rolls the car. He died at the hospital two hours later. Gladys blames herself. "If only I hadn't shouted at him, he'd still be alive," she said then, still does.'

'Not her fault.'

'I know that but try convincing her. The Blatchfords and that Gloria Wiggins were in her ear from that day on, saying that she will find comfort in the Bible, and she believes it.'

'What's she like with you now?'

'She's cold, distant. Before she was an affectionate woman. Nowadays she goes her way, I go mine. I'll tell you, two out of three dead is not a bad result. Whoever it was, he's got my vote,' Upminster said.

'It could have been you.'

'It could have been, except it wasn't. No alibi if that's what you're after, but I wouldn't have killed them.'

'Why?'

'I've no problem with death as I have to slaughter the occasional pig or sheep up at the farm, but a human being, that's different.'

'Your dislike of them is a motive,' Tremayne said as he ate his steak and kidney pie.

'It is, and if Sheila Blatchford meets the same fate, it won't be me shedding a tear.'

'Your wife?'

'Have you ever lost a child, Tremayne?' Upminster said.

'I've never had children,' Tremayne admitted, but regretted that he had not.

'When one of them dies, even if he or she's not a good person, it tears you to pieces, inside and out. In time, the sorrow goes away, it did with me, but it took nearly a year. With Gladys, it never did, and there was a time when I had to contemplate placing her somewhere safe.'

'Such as?'

'A home for the mentally unstable. Her grief was inconsolable, irrational, and downright harmful. If it hadn't been for that Wiggins woman and the Blatchfords, Gladys wouldn't have made it. Not that it stops me hating them and wishing them dead.'

'But your wife?'

'With time and the right care, she would have recovered, I'm sure of that, but for a while I was concerned that she would harm herself.'

'Drastic measures, putting her away for some time,' Tremayne acknowledged. He had to admit to enjoying Upminster's company, so much so that he ordered the two of them another pint of beer. Clare was not finding her company so agreeable. She had joined the fire and brimstone brigade in the other corner.

***

'That's the problem with people today,' Sheila Blatchford said, focussing on Clare. 'You place your trust in what you can see and feel. Now, look here at Sergeant Yarwood, no offence intended.' Clare knew there was, but she was not there to debate.

Of the others at the table, all would profess to their sadness at Gloria Wiggins' death, but that did not obviate them from her murder. And Bert Blatchford's recent death should have been a dampener, especially with his widow, yet it appeared to have little effect.

'You're right,' Margaret Wilmot said. 'The two police officers here in this pub expect to find out what happened to Gloria and to Sheila's husband, when the truth is out there, amongst the sinners. None of us would have killed them, but they look at us as if we were akin to the devil, when all any of us wanted to do was to protect this community.'

'Rupert Baxter?' Clare said.

'His time will come,' Sheila said.

'What about Gloria Wiggins and your husband?'

'My Bert was a weak man, couldn't hold his drink, nor his tongue.'

'What does that mean? We know about his drinking, but not his tongue. Were you frightened that he would have said something about Gloria if we had kept probing? Was his silence a necessary price to pay? Could one of you seated at this table have killed him?'

Hamish Foster, who until now had been sitting back enjoying the spectacle, put his glass down on the table and spoke. 'My wife and I have perfect alibis,' he said.

'And what are they?'

'We weren't in the village at either time, and that's verifiable,' Foster said, looking over at his wife, who nodded her head in agreement.

Clare knew that solid alibis were always open to conjecture. Being at home watching the television was not sufficient, and being at the cinema in Salisbury, about a twenty-minute drive away, was not either.

'Where were you?'

'In London, at our son's. He'll provide our alibi.'

Stephanie Underwood walked into the pub. Tremayne and Clare realised she was a nosy woman, and if it was information that she required, then where better than the pub. She ordered a drink and sat down at the bar. Clare could see her ears pricking as she strained to listen to the various conversations in the pub.

Tremayne looked over at the woman, then at Clare, a slight lifting of his eyebrows. Clare understood. If her hearing was that good, how come she had not heard the commotion from next door when her neighbour had been murdered. Even if Gloria Wiggins had been unconscious, it would have required some effort to move her to the garage, unless there were two people, but Jim Hughes and his CSIs had discounted that possibility.

Clare left where she was sitting and moved over to the bar. She was still holding her first glass of wine, Tremayne was on his third pint of beer. It was good that she was driving, and not him.

'Sergeant Yarwood, I'm surprised to see you here,' Stephanie Underwood said.

'DI Tremayne always reckons the local pub is the best place for candid conversation,' Clare said. Baxter came over, interested to know if either of the ladies wanted another drink; both declined.

'I don't come that often, but the mood in the village is strange. Even at home, I could feel it.'

'What do you mean?'

'Impending doom. As if it's not over yet.'

'Someone else will die, is that it?'

'It's a small village with big secrets.'

'Most villages in the area have them, and once the equilibrium is broken, then emotions run unchecked, deaths occur.'

'Gloria, I could understand, but Bert, he wasn't so bad. Why did he die, do you know?' Stephanie asked.

'We were looking for a common motive, but maybe there isn't one,' Clare said. 'Murder's a serious crime committed by people for a myriad of reasons. Gloria's may have been for her venomous denouncing of others in the village, but Bert makes no sense. A drunk, and a zealot, but, by and large, he minded his own business.'

'Bert was whatever Sheila told him to be. Outside of their farm, he pretended to be in charge, but he wasn't. For whatever reason, he was devoted to Sheila, not that she deserved it, but each to their own, I suppose.'

'How about you?' Clare asked. 'No man in your life?'

'Never has been. Not that I wasn't interested, especially as a teen at school in Salisbury. A few turns around the back of the bike shed, but it wasn't something that drove me. After school, I realised that I didn't need a man, and I've been content to just stay here. Too many people rushing here and there, getting ulcers, destroying their lives by chasing the wrong person, sleeping with the wrong one on occasion. You know about Rupert and Sheila?'

'We do.'

'I remember his father, a likeable rogue.'

'Any problems with him?'

'He used to look me up and down when I was in my teens, but no, nothing more. Rupert and his brother, both decent men, as well. I fancied Rupert when he was younger, back of the bike shed with him once, but it was a long time ago, I doubt if he remembers.'

'You can be certain he does,' Clare said.

'I was attractive back then, and it was what teens did, even if they weren't too keen. I remember Rupert's wife, a severe woman, not a lot of humour about her. I don't think I ever saw her smile once, and their son, he was only young then, but he wasn't what you'd call a lovely baby, but I suppose parents see them differently.'

'They do.'

'And how about you, Sergeant?' The patter of little feet back at home?'

'Not for me, not yet,' Clare responded, realising that she had sat with the woman to gain information, not to discuss her life. 'Tell me more about Gloria Wiggins? What was she like as a neighbour? As a friend?'

'As a neighbour, she was fine. I like everything to be in its place, and with her, there were never any disputes over one of us not tidying up or having loud parties. I don't think she had a true friend in the world, and certainly not me. She may have been friendly with Sheila Blatchford and her people, but that was only because of a united cause.'

'What cause?'

'The malignant kind, the sort that upsets people. Sheila revels in it, so did Gloria.'

'Did she believe all that she s said?'

'She did. Rupert's brother was on the end of it once, and they've been into Rupert on more than one occasion, but he's a stronger character than his brother. Effeminate, he was, but then you must know that.'

'Homosexual?'

'They called him a sodomite, more damning than the words they use today. It used to upset him, and Rupert used to tell him to stand up to them, but that wasn't his nature. His motorbike was probably the only sanctity that he could find, unfortunate that it killed him in the end.'

'Who else have they levelled their vindictiveness against?'

'Everyone who's upset them, which in this village has meant virtually everyone. At least they're democratic.'

'And you?'

'They've tried, but I'm made of sterner stuff. That's why I got on with Gloria. I didn't like her, nor her me, but we could sit down over a cup of tea and have a chat.'

'We found her husband,' Clare said. Stephanie Underwood paused before speaking again.

'We always thought him to be a creation of her imagination. Tell me about him.'

'He's alive and married. They were married for a short time, and he only visited this village once, and then only for a few minutes. Could it have had any bearing on her death and that of Bert Blatchford?'

'Why? Should it?'

'I was asking the question,' Clare said. She broke her cardinal rule and ordered another glass of wine, prosecco for her talkative companion.

'Everyone called her Mrs Wiggins, whether they believed that she had been married or not. It made no difference to the people here, only to her. Is he coming here? Did he leave her? What was he like?'

'A lot of questions, Miss Underwood.'

'Stephanie, please.'

'Very well. Stephanie. I can tell you that she left him and subsequently divorced. They were not married for very long, and after so many years, he does not have any strong feelings for her one way or another. It is unlikely that he will come here, and he has an alibi for the time that she died. Unless we receive information to the contrary, he is not part of our enquiry.'

'Then it's someone in this village.'

'It probably is. Why didn't you hear any commotion next door?'

'Gloria was always rattling around in her place. Ten in the evening and she would still be making a noise. Not the sort you could complain about, but it was the time for quiet, not banging this and that. Over the years, I've tuned her out. Maybe I did hear a commotion, but my subconscious would have muted the sound. It's the same as with a barking dog. It drives you crazy at first, but then after a few months, you can barely hear the animal.'

Clare could not fault the reasoning behind the woman's answer. Stephanie Underwood, fuelled by new gossip regarding the mysterious husband, left and walked up the road to her cottage. Clare knew she'd be stopping on the way to pass on the latest news.

Leaving the bar, Clare walked over to Tremayne and Eustace Upminster. She could see that the two of them were showing the early effects of one-too-many pints of beer. Over in the other corner, Sheila Blatchford was still holding court, her attentive admirers giving her attention. Hamish Foster looked as though he was bored with what was being said, although his wife, Desdemona, was still enthralled.

Clare could see an uneven matching in the Fosters. The husband was tall, physically strong, not the sort of man to tolerate a bigoted woman such as Sheila Blatchford, not the kind of man to be hanging onto his wife's apron strings, which appeared to be the case. Gladys Upminster, a woman in late middle age, and still attractive in an earthy, fresh-aired way, with the look of someone who lived in the country and spent a lot of time outside, sat calmly, focussed on Sheila, casting the occasional disparaging glance towards her husband, the sort of look that Clare recognised as a 'wait till I get you home and give you a lashing of my tongue' look.

Chapter 9

The news that Gloria Wiggins had been married spread like wildfire in the small community of Compton, so much so that Clare had some reservations in the following days as to whether it had been a good move on her part to tell Stephanie Underwood. Tremayne saw it differently. As far as he was concerned an unknown element had been brought into the investigation, and although Cuthbert Wiggins had only visited once, and as he had said, only for five minutes, it raised speculation. The local gossips were in full flow discussing the unexpected titbit, some stating that they had seen him more than once in the village. If that was true, and Gloria Wiggins' former husband had been in the village on more than one occasion, then he had lied, and he was a prime suspect.

Apart from the man who professed to have loved the woman once, no one else was coming forward in Compton with anything other than derision and scathing comments about a person who caused more harm than good, who had a sharp tongue and the ability to make the most righteous and fair-minded villager sound akin to a devil worshipper.

Tremayne sat pensively in his office, a sure sign that he was reviewing the case.

Clare gave him five more minutes before she entered and sat opposite him. 'What's the plan?' she said, knowing full well that her senior was never short of an idea on how to proceed.

'We're focussing on Gloria at the expense of Blatchford,' he said.

'She's the catalyst.'

'Even if Wiggins had visited the village on more than one occasion, even if he had killed Gloria, it doesn't tie in with Bert Blatchford, or does it?'

'What do we know about Bert, about bank manager Wiggins, about anyone? We only know what they let us see. Maybe Wiggins had spent time there, and Gloria knew this.'

'But why? You've checked out the divorce from her husband. What he said was true. She cleaned the man out, so why would he keep in contact?'

'He could have visited without her knowing,' Clare said. 'Still more unknowns, another village with more secrets than people. The answers lie in the village, not at the police station.'

'Too many variables. Cuthbert Wiggins is still a long shot at this time. Let's focus on the village. There are enough people who didn't like the dead woman, more than enough that didn't like Bert Blatchford.'

'There are even more who didn't like Blatchford's wife. She could be the next victim.'

'We'd better go and talk to her, let her know the situation.'

Tremayne, glad to be out his office, did not like the Blatchfords' farm. He was a city man, and even though Salisbury was small, centred on a twelfth-century cathedral and a modest population, it still represented normality to him. Traipsing around in the mud, even up to the front of the Blatchfords' farmhouse, did not improve his mood. He had met enough narrow-minded people over the years, and he knew that Sheila Blatchford was not going to be an easy woman to question.

Clare knocked on the door, although not expecting a reply, assuming that the woman would be out on the farm. It was not large, no more than fifty acres, and was scruffy with a down-at-heel look. Over on one side, closer to the road that passed the village, stood the pigsty where Bert had died. On another side, one hundred yards from the road, an old and rusty tractor decayed. One of its tyres was flat, a sure sign that it had not moved in a long time. A barn door was open next to it.

'She's probably over there,' Clare said. She had grown up near the countryside in Norfolk. She liked being on a farm, even one as unappealing as the Blatchfords'. She savoured the smell in the air, the chickens walking around the farm, the ducks over in one corner, the geese, raucous at the best of times, deafening at others. And now they were in full chorus, enough to wake the dead Tremayne would have said, if asked.

The two police officers walked across to the barn and peered inside. The smell of hay and animals, but no sign of the woman in question.

'She's not here,' Tremayne said.

'Her car's outside. She'll not be far,' Clare said.

Clare walked around the barn, taking care to avoid the animals' calling cards that littered the floor. Up high on one of the rafters, two pigeons. The barn was dark and damp, and Clare felt unease as she continued to look. Tremayne had left the building to look around outside, but primarily because he needed a cigarette. With Clare and Jean in his ear, he had cut down to five a day, yet the need for more remained.

Tremayne lit his cigarette and walked around the farmyard. Inside the car, he could see the keys, the woman's handbag on the passenger seat. Nothing unusual in itself as people still left their doors open in Compton. He completed a circuit of the outside of the barn before returning to its door.

'Yarwood, are you still in there?' No answer. He called again, this time louder. '*Are you still in there?*'

'Over here,' a weak voice replied. 'Come quick.'

Tremayne walked through the barn, faster than his usual pace, stepping in horse manure, cursing at the time, concerned about what Yarwood had found or what she was up to. He found her sitting on a bale of hay; she had vomited.

'Too much farm air,' he said flippantly as he saw her discomfort.

'Around the back. Take a look, if you can.'

Tremayne pushed through the bales of hay where Clare had indicated. It was a tight squeeze for him to get through. He saw what had caused his sergeant to vomit. He could feel the bile in his throat, and he took out his handkerchief to hold against his mouth and to press against his nose to moderate the smell. 'Jesus Christ,' he said.

At his rear, Clare stood, not looking directly at the scene in front of them. There on the floor, the remains of Sheila Blatchford.

'How can anyone do this sort of thing?' Clare said.

Tremayne, who had seen more than Clare in his thirty-plus years with the police force, knew the answer. People are capable of anything, although this was the work of a sadist or a person feeling extreme hatred. The body of Sheila Blatchford had been carved up with a chainsaw that was lying to one side. The area was full of blood and it squelched underneath their feet. Flies, large and voracious, were settled on the body, the air alive with more of them. The two police officers retreated back down the narrow alley by which they had entered. Clare took out her phone and called Jim Hughes.

'Blatchfords' farm,' she said.

'Another one?' Hughes' reply.

'Sheila Blatchford, or at least we think it is.'

'You're not sure?'

'She's been butchered, and she's been stewing in the barn for some time. Don't bring any of your juniors. It'll turn their stomachs.'

'Yours?'

'Mine, and DI Tremayne's looking green around the gills.'

'I'll be there in twenty-five minutes; the team should be there within ninety. You'll be establishing the crime scene?'

'I'll get a couple of uniforms to set it up. Tremayne and I will be here on your arrival. Be prepared to be shocked.'

Outside of the barn, Tremayne lit another cigarette. It was over his quota, but Clare didn't offer any comment; now was not the time for light-hearted repartee. It was now a crime scene, and whereas both Gloria Wiggins and Bert Blatchford had met violent deaths, they were nothing compared to the savagery inflicted on Sheila Blatchford.

'Was she alive when whoever it was started?' Clare asked, more by way of affirmation that she was not, rather than seeking a precise answer.

'That's up to the crime scene team and the pathologist to tell us. Judging by the blood, it's a possibility.'

'Someone in the village?'

'But why reserve that for her? It looks as if the fire and brimstoners are the targets, which can only mean that anyone else associated with them is a possible victim. Once we're finished here, we'll bring them together at the pub. Judging by the village, no one else has sensed what's going on.'

'They will once the crime scene investigators arrive. I could do with a drink to calm my nerves,' Clare said.

'Phone up Rupert Baxter, get him to come down with a couple of hot drinks.'

'And what will you be doing?'

'Kitting up in coveralls and shoe covers, the same as you. No point in making our presence any more visible than it already is.'

Baxter arrived within ten minutes, a flask and two cups in his hands. He had parked a hundred yards back and walked down in accordance with the instructions he had received. Clare could see a crowd forming closer to the pub.

'News travels fast,' Baxter said.

'It does if you tell them,' Tremayne replied.

'You phoned the pub. It was busy, some of the locals overheard. And besides, what is it?'

'Sheila Blatchford. She's been murdered.'

'After Gloria and Bert, it seemed a possibility.'

'That's what we thought. That's why we came looking for her, to warn her.'

'Too late, I assume.'

'Too late.' Clare could see Baxter fishing for information, something to take back to the pub. A police car arrived, two uniforms set to work securing the area. Jim Hughes was not far behind. He took one look in the barn and came out, not smiling as he had been when he had entered.

'That's too much for me,' he said.

Baxter, all ears, took in what was being said. 'This is not for repeating at the pub,' Tremayne said, knowing that it would be.

'They'll ask.'

'Tell them that Sheila Blatchford is dead. No mention of what Hughes just said.'

'Violent?'

'We'll be up later to talk to those who were part of the woman's inner circle.'

'Some are not here.'

'Who and where?'

'Hamish and Desdemona Foster went into Salisbury this morning.'

'Yarwood, make a phone call. Get them back here. Baxter, you have their phone number?'

'I do.'

'Very well. Give it to Yarwood. Forty-five minutes at the pub, and that doesn't mean the whole village, just those closest to the woman, is that understood?'

'I'll arrange it,' Baxter said.

No longer were they looking for a murderer, now they were looking for a psychopath, someone capable of extreme barbarism, and worst of all, someone who was a

valued member of the community. Tremayne realised that
they were dealing with the most dangerous of individuals,
someone with the mental acumen to confuse a police
investigation.

Once again, a single murder had brought out a
serial killer, someone who kills for a reason, although that
reason still remained unclear.

Hughes and his crime scene team mobilised at the
Blatchfords' farm. Tremayne and Clare received a
preliminary report from Hughes to confirm that Sheila
Blatchford had been killed before being butchered, a cord
around her neck showing that she had been strangled.
Also, the time of death had been estimated at twenty-four
to thirty-six hours previous to the body's discovery, the
time based on the temperature of the body and the
congealing blood, as well as the flies. Jim Hughes was
hopeful of tightening up on the hour of the death, and
Pathology still had to complete a thorough investigation
of the body.

At the pub, Sheila Blatchford's group sat in their
usual corner and Rupert Baxter was behind the bar, with
Stephanie Underwood perched on the other side. Baxter
had made sure that everyone had a drink and had paid for
it. Clare looked at those assembled. Margaret Wilmot
maintained her impassive facial expression: dull,
disinterested, eyes focussed forward and not at the police
officers. Gladys Upminster was in tears, not unexpected
in that she had used Sheila Blatchford and the two others
who had been murdered as her support after the death of
her son. Her husband sat where he had been when he and
Tremayne had drunk a few too many beers. Hamish and
Desdemona Foster sat one table distant from the other
fire and brimstoners. Yet again, Desdemona was in a
floral dress, although her face did not reflect the sunny

disposition of her clothing. Hamish Foster sat back on his chair; he was holding a pint of beer.

If Clare and Tremayne had had to take a guess at what his face was hiding, it would be that he was not too upset that a woman had died. However, both of the police officers knew that appearances could be deceiving. Sheila Blatchford had shown little distress at her husband's death, although they were apparently very close, yet they were known to argue at times, even hitting each other on more than one occasion.

'Sorry, Miss Underwood, not this time,' Clare said, as she ushered the woman out of the pub. The local gossip would have to find out from a third party if she wanted to tell the village, and Rupert Baxter was not beyond spreading the news.

The death of Sheila Blatchford was common knowledge in the village, with a crowd down by the farm, a few more outside the pub. Tremayne took a long, hard look at all those in the pub, attempted to see any signs of arduous scrubbing of their bodies, the typical reaction of most people after being confronted by so much blood. He could see none.

Tremayne sat down with those assembled. 'Sheila Blatchford has been murdered,' he said.

'We've been told,' Margaret Wilmot said. It was the first time that Tremayne had heard her speak. The detective inspector remembered Baxter saying that she was back from the dead.

'Was it violent?' The woman spoke for the second time.

'It was. We'll need your alibis and separate interviews and statements.'

'He did it,' Margaret Wilmot said, turning around on her chair and pointing at Rupert Baxter.

'Just because I don't hold with them and because of James and his leanings, they always want to blame me,' Baxter said.

'It's him, I'm telling you,' Margaret Wilmot said. She was on her feet, moving towards Baxter.

If looks could kill, he'd be dead by now, Clare thought.

Clare moved into the woman's path. 'Please sit down. We're conducting a murder investigation here, not indulging in idle accusations. Or do you have proof?'

'I've seen him down there when Bert wasn't around. I know what was going on.'

'If what you are saying is true, and that Mr Baxter and Mrs Blatchford were having an affair, why did you side with her? Both would be equally guilty of sin.'

'Sheila's heart was pure; Rupert Baxter's is not.'

'You didn't forgive James Baxter. Surely he must have had a pure heart.'

'To err is human, but not what he was doing with Barry Woodcock. I saw the two of them that day, both naked, indulging in sin, mocking the Lord, and not far from the church. It was wicked, inhuman, worthy of burning at the stake. Sheila Blatchford was a righteous woman, seduced by a known lecher. Oh, yes, I know about his father and Sheila's mother. We all did, not that you'd know if you ever met them in the street.'

'You're willing to forgive Sheila, but not Rupert. Why is he the murderer?'

'She was getting clingy, wanting to leave Bert, move in with him behind the bar. We know what he is like. Others had fallen for his charm, erred onto the path of evil.'

'Have you?' Clare asked.

'I cannot answer that question,' Margaret Wilmot said.

'It's either here or down at the police station.'
Clare looked over at Rupert Baxter, saw that he was
trying to stay out of her direct view. 'Mr Baxter, the truth.
Were you involved with Sheila, with Margaret Wilmot?'

'She's right on one count,' Baxter said.

'You were involved with Sheila Blatchford.'

'No. But I was with Margaret when we were
younger. Not such a sour old prune back then and
attractive in a wholesome way. We were lovers, although
she'd rather forget, and I've never said anything since
then about it to anyone.'

'Sheila Blatchford?'

'You know of my relationship with her, so does
everyone else in this bar. She was my half-sister. There
was a bond between us. I used to go and see her
occasionally, just to talk, to reflect on life and the
different paths it had taken us. I did not like the woman,
nor could I hate her. It was the same for her, the typical
dysfunctional family.'

'If she hadn't been related?' Clare asked.

'Take away the nonsense she used to spout, she
was a good woman, hardworking, loyal, and she deserved
better than Bert Blatchford. The man was a worthless
lump of lard.'

'Yet, Mr Baxter,' Tremayne interjected, 'you do
not seem to be concerned that she has died violently.
Why is that?'

'For now, one of the persecutors of my brother is
dead. My emotions are confused. I should be sad, but I
am not. And as for Margaret, a lovely woman in her time,
she was nothing compared to Sheila. For a while, I could
see a future with her, but then she went and married
Chris Wilmot, a timid man, nagged him into his grave.
Thankfully, I missed out on married bliss with Margaret.

But let me say this, Margaret is a woman who can hate, and don't assume that she or any of those in the corner is innocent of murder.'

'You were Gloria's age,' Clare said.

'When Gloria was younger, the same as with Stephanie, the same as with Margaret, but it was a long time ago.'

'Mrs Wilmot, have you anything to say?' Clare said.

'No, not for now. I want to go back to my house.'

'Unfortunately, we need to take statements,' Tremayne said. The meeting at the pub had gone better than expected. The inevitable skeletons were surfacing, yet there were more, Tremayne knew, and if one of those who were sitting in the pub was the murderer, then he or she was playing with them, and enjoying every moment.

Chapter 10

Apart from a friendship with James Baxter in the past, Barry Woodcock gave no hint that his leanings were anything other than aimed at his wife, a woman who exuded an earthy countryside charm.

Tremayne and Clare arrived at the Woodcocks' small farm early in the morning. The air was crisp and the grass, with an early morning frost on it, crackled as they walked over the lawn to the front door. The house had a lived-in look, and apart from a broken window pane in one of the upstairs windows, it was not unattractive.

'What can I do for you?' Gwen Woodcock shouted from the front door. She was dressed in clothes suited for indoors, and her arms were wrapped around her body to keep warm.

'A few questions, Mrs Woodcock,' Tremayne's reply. There was no need to state who he and Clare were, having met the woman in the village before, although then it had only been an introduction. Now, it was time to interview her.

'Very well, come in. Barry's out in the fields.' A cigarette drooped from the woman's mouth, its ash about to drop off.

Inside the house, neat and tidy, the furniture was functional, the décor rudimentary, although the air was heavy with the smell of tobacco. The two police officers took off the heavy coats they were wearing. A roaring log fire burnt in the hearth of the open fireplace. The youngest child played with its toys, the other two children were not visible.

'Mrs Woodcock, we need a statement from you,' Clare said.

'Gwen. Mrs Woodcock makes me sound old.'

'Very well. Three people have died so far, and your husband has stated that he was with you on all three occasions.'

'That would be correct, but if you're looking for proof, there isn't any. We're not great socialisers, although Barry has the occasional drink at the pub; apart from that, we don't travel far.'

'Did you have any reason to hate any of the three that have died?'

'Not really. Gloria was an interfering busybody, but I gave her no credence. She said some scurrilous remarks about Barry and James Baxter in the past, and the Blatchfords were hardly the salt of the earth. Bert was harmless most of the time, although a bad drunk, and Sheila, a good worker, made good jam. She kept Bert on the straight and narrow and I wouldn't have given you tuppence for her, but murder, that's something different.'

'Are you sad that they've died?' Tremayne asked. He liked a person who said their mind and wasn't always politically correct. With Gwen Woodcock smoking in the house, he felt inclined to light up, but he did not.

'Should I?'

'You grew up around here, the same as them.'

'Apart from what they said about Barry and the vicar, I tried to ignore them. I focus on my family; anyone else is on the periphery, at least as far as I'm concerned.'

'The strongest motive for their deaths is revenge, which makes your husband the primary suspect,' Tremayne said.

So far, Gwen Woodcock, even if she was not a person to warm to with her offhand manner, had been straight with Tremayne and Clare. Outside in the yard, Barry's old Land Rover. A dog slept close to the fire, its breed indeterminable.

'I know my husband,' Gwen said. 'We went to school together, and then when we were old enough, we were dating, not that there was anywhere to go of a night. The cinema on a Saturday night, and we were still too young for the pub, although I'm not keen on alcohol, but Barry sometimes has one or two more than he should, but then, men always do.'

Tremayne knew what she meant. He was rationed to three pints of a night, and he still hankered after five and twice as many cigarettes. But after the scare when he had drunk too much, smoked too much, and no doubt eaten too much, and then the night in the hospital, the doctor had made it clear that it was either moderate his habits or a wooden box six feet under. Tremayne had reluctantly chosen to follow instructions, though he didn't have many options, what with Jean at home and Yarwood in the office, and the two of them comparing notes.

'No truth in the rumour, is that what you're saying? You must realise that the truth will come out eventually,' Clare said.

'I'm not defending my husband from scurrilous gossip. Those who indulge in character assassinations are not as clean as they pretend to be. I could tell you about some of them, especially Sheila Blatchford. But she's dead, and it doesn't pay to talk badly of the departed.'

'Why would someone kill them after so many years?'

'How would I know? I remember when James Baxter died. Barry was upset, but then he had been friends with the man, and he was at the church every Sunday, the same as I was.'

'Nowadays?'

'Not often. The children were baptised there, and the eldest two are at Sunday school. Does them no harm and the Reverend Tichborne is a decent man.'

'Why not every Sunday?'

'We're too busy, what with the children and the farm. As you can see, we're not exactly brimming with money, and a day off, even a Sunday morning, is not on our schedule. We'll make an exception to take the children to the doctor if it's needed, but apart from that, our lives are too full. And besides, Tichborne can make a sermon sound like a dirge, and as for Gloria and the others, they would only make veiled comments about the rest of us. Barry took no notice, but I did. Gloria had money but she never gave it to anyone else, yet she was thick with the Blatchfords, and look what it got them, Bert with a knife in his back, Sheila cut up with a Ryobi chainsaw.'

'We never mentioned the make of the chainsaw,' Tremayne said.

'Lucky guess, and anyway, what other make is there if you want to do some serious sawing?'

'Do you have a chainsaw?'

'Under lock and key. I caught the eldest fooling around with it one day. He thought it was a lightsabre or something else silly. Too much nonsense on the television, not that they watch it often.'

'How often?' Clare said.

'At the weekends, Saturday afternoon. I know it's not ideal for them to watch, but they're good children so I give them some slack. The boy, he's into science fiction, the girl, she likes silly and soppy. The baby doesn't care for either, but he enjoys being there with them.'

'Coming back to your chainsaw,' Tremayne said.

'Under lock and key, not that we use it much. Barry's keen on the old ways, and he takes part in those log sawing competitions that you see at the agricultural fairs. He's won a few prizes over the years. He's good for firewood for the fire and the stove in the house.'

'Can we look at your chainsaw?' Clare asked.

'It's in a shed out back. No one's been in there, and it hasn't been used for over a year.'

'Nevertheless, we'd still like to see it.'

Tremayne sensed a hesitancy in the woman. There was no reason to suspect her of any crime, but the savagery inflicted on Sheila Blatchford showed a person skilled at wielding a chainsaw, a person such as Barry Woodcock.

Outside the house a track led over to an old wooden shed. In keeping with the farm in general it was functional, sturdy, but had no beauty about it, even though it was over two hundred years old. The double doors at the front were secured by a large padlock. Gwen Woodcock turned the key in the lock. She placed the lock to one side and opened one of the doors, its hinges creaking.

Inside, a musty place of damp and decay. An old plough rusted to one side, an old bench stood on the other, complete with tools, mostly old and no longer usable.

The woman indicated a big metal chest. However, it was not locked. Clare made a phone call to Jim Hughes and his crime scene team to come out to the Woodcocks' farm as soon as possible. Tremayne put on a pair of gloves that he carried in his pocket. He opened the lid of the chest to find it empty.

'Now we know where the chainsaw came from that chopped up Sheila Blatchford,' Tremayne said.

'It can't be Barry. He's not capable of hurting anyone,' Gwen said.

'I'm afraid this doesn't look good for your husband. Not only is your chainsaw the probable murder weapon, but your husband has the strength and the ability to wield the instrument. You, Mrs Woodcock, are not strong enough.'

'Barry will have an explanation, I know he will.'

'You defended him over his relationship with James Baxter. Are you now going to defend him if he is a person with a motive and the ability?'

'I'll always defend him. It's called loyalty, but he didn't kill any of the three. I know it.'

'Do you, Mrs Woodcock?' Clare said.

'Yes.'

'If your husband is guilty of the murder of Sheila Blatchford, it presents a complication,' Tremayne said.

'What do you mean?' Gwen said. She was sitting on an old chair, looking at the empty chest. If, as she had said, she trusted her husband implicitly, did the missing chainsaw indicate another side to the man, an unknown element, violence, a need for revenge? Clare had trusted a former lover in much the same way, only to find out that he was a murderer who had then died while trying to save her. Was Gwen Woodcock in the same situation? A woman misled by a husband, a man she thought she knew, but now wasn't so sure about.

'Gloria Wiggins was lifted up using a pulley system. If your husband is a murderer, the murderer of Gloria Wiggins, then why would he have used the pulleys? He's a strong man, more than capable of pulling the woman up with his bare hands.'

'Two murderers?' Clare said.

'It's possible. A family united, is that what the Woodcocks are?' Tremayne said, fully aware that he was baiting a woman who was visibly stunned by what had been found in the old shed.

Chapter 11

Barry Woodcock was not pleased when told of the harassment his wife had been subjected to over the missing chainsaw. Jim Hughes and his team checked the chest where it had been stored, confirmed that the oil residue found in the empty space and the oil found in the murder weapon were one and the same. Tremayne knew that raised additional questions, especially for Barry, who would gladly have hit Tremayne if he hadn't been a serving police officer. It had been Barry's wife, temporarily distracted by her husband's anger, who calmed the situation. One of the children wandered into the room due to the commotion and immediately went to its mother. Gwen Woodcock gave the child a hug and took it back to its room.

Clare remembered that her mother had always been restrained in her affections, but her father had compensated. But in the Woodcock household, it was equal love from both of the parents. Clare hoped that Barry and Gwen Woodcock were not guilty of any crimes, but as Tremayne had told her on many occasions, it's not whether they are good or bad people, it's whether they are innocent or guilty. Their job as police officers is to get to the truth, charge the guilty, ensure a conviction, and don't stuff up in the meantime.

Clare knew what he had meant, agreed with him totally, but sometimes she wished it wasn't that way.

'If, as you say, you and your wife are innocent, then why your chainsaw? It would be easy enough to make a case against you, though circumstantial mainly,' Tremayne said.

'My Barry wouldn't harm anyone,' Gwen Woodcock said on her return from calming her child in its room.

'As you've said,' Clare said. She had to sympathise with the woman, but Tremayne had been attempting to break through the typical country folks' reticence, of which Gwen Woodcock showed plenty. Barry Woodcock's emotional outburst, his reddening face, were not indicative of his usual demeanour. It had been Baxter, the publican, who had said that even after his brother, James, had died that eventful night after Gloria Wiggins' venomous accusations, Barry's reaction had been to stifle any emotional outbreak, although he had cried at the funeral, had even carried the coffin, and spoken one of James's favourite passages from the Bible.

But not once, Baxter had been adamant on that fact, had Barry Woodcock confronted Gloria Wiggins, nor Bert Blatchford and his wife.

'It's not an open and shut case,' Tremayne said, 'but I could make it stick. What do you say about that? Do you want me to pursue a warrant for your arrest, slam you both in the cells at Bemerton Road Police Station, put your children in care?'

'We can't tell you more,' Gwen Woodcock said. 'Barry's innocent, and so am I. The lock not being on the chest is suspicious, I'll agree, but neither of us had been in that shed recently, and the door was locked at the front. Maybe around the back you'll find a way in, but it wasn't us, and we didn't give the chainsaw to anyone.'

'DI Tremayne is throwing you a lifeline,' Clare said. She was sitting down on an old wooden chair, the sort that looks as though it belongs to a house in the country, the sort that was uncomfortable. She stood up and moved closer to the heat from the fire. She turned her back to it and enjoyed the relief from the biting cold that was creeping under the back door.

'There's no more we can say,' Barry Woodcock said. He had his arm around his wife. The investigation had changed from accusatory to consultative. Tremayne and Clare needed something to move the investigation forward. There were other police inspectors, Clare knew, who would have seized on the possibility of an arrest, taken the easy way out, but that wasn't Tremayne's style.

'Tell us about the others,' Clare said.

'Which others?'

'Margaret Wilmot, Eustace and Gladys Upminster, Hamish and Desdemona Foster.'

'Margaret, you know. A decent woman when she was younger, but now difficult.'

'Capable of murder?'

'It's hard to say with that woman. She doesn't give you much to go with, and what she's thinking, you'd never know. I don't think she liked any of those who are dead, certain she doesn't like anyone or anything, other than the mangy cat that she calls her pet.'

'Why mangy?' Clare said.

'I was up there not so long ago,' Gwen said. 'The cat must be sixteen years old, yet it sits there looking you up and down. It's almost as if it knows what you're thinking.'

'Does it?'

'Who knows? Not that I'd give any credence to the cat, black it is, but you know.'

'I don't think we do,' Clare said.

'There are some who believe this story about her death some years back, somehow attribute something unnatural to it.'

'Do you?'

'Not me. As far as I'm concerned, the cat is black, and it was modern medical practices that brought her back, nothing more.'

'So, you're up there,' Tremayne said. 'You don't like the woman, yet you go and socialise with her. It makes no sense.'

'This farm belongs to her. You'd not know it looking at the woman, but Margaret Wilmot is the richest person in this village by far. She lives in a sixteenth-century manor house. It should be a historic property, but it's falling down around her ears. One day soon they won't have to wonder whether she's dead or alive. The roof will cave in, and she'll be underneath it when it falls. Not that we'll complain or express any sympathy.'

Clare had to admire that frankness of the Woodcocks, but they were not helping their case. Circumstantial evidence instead of concrete facts could be damning, and at the end of the day, there were three murders, all in need of a murderer. And two people were talking themselves into that position.

'That's how I was brought up,' Gwen continued. 'My parents, good people, called a spade a spade. They wouldn't have held with this modern idea of political correctness where you have to watch what you say and do. They're dead now, worked themselves into an early grave, and that Wilmot woman didn't help, so don't ask me to pretend to care when I don't.'

'And if Margaret Wilmot dies?' Tremayne asked.

'You'll check, no doubt,' Barry Woodcock said.

'We will.'

'The Wilmots have had influence in this village since the seventeenth century. Back then we were the peasants, but not now. We have the same rights as them, and legislation over the centuries has given us a claim on this farm. It's to do with the Wilmots not adhering to what was passed into law in the last hundred years. We've got a solicitor looking into it, and our claim, including the fact that the Wilmots overcharged us in the past, makes a strong case for us to take this land from the woman's estate on her death. We may have to pay some money, but it'll be a nominal amount.'

'Yet again, you'd benefit if another person dies.'

'We would, but it doesn't make us murderers.'

'We've no other obvious suspects. Rupert Baxter had a reason to want them dead, but his alibi, at least for one of the murders, is strong, whereas yours aren't. Eustace and Gladys Upminster, what can you tell us about them?'

'Eustace is a good man. He's got no axe to grind, and they own their farm. Gladys changed after the death of her son. She was always headstrong, but it unhinged her. She found solace with Gloria, and then Sheila.'

'Eustace seems to be a strong-willed man,' Clare said.

'That's what you see. We suspect that Gladys controls him. She came from money, he didn't. It was her father who staked the money for their farm, although now it's been paid back. We've no idea of the terms that were agreed, or whether the farm's in Gladys's name, or in both.'

'Hamish and Desdemona Foster?'

'Desdemona's easily led. Hamish is devoted to her. There's not much more to say about either of them. I can't see either of them as being capable of murder.'

'We need the truth about you and James Baxter,' Tremayne said.

'The relationship between myself and James had been strong, but it was not physical, although James may have preferred it to be. However, I wasn't interested, and James was a man of great restraint.'

'What does that mean?'

'What do you think it means? The man was gay, no reason for him to be ashamed of the fact, but he answered to superiors, more than likely the bishop in Salisbury, and he would not have approved. James was, after all, a man devoted to this community, always helping those in trouble, always being available to the sick and elderly. He wouldn't have done anything to jeopardise his calling.'

'Then why did Gloria Wiggins say that she had seen you and him?'

'Margaret said it first, and then Gloria latched on to the story and ran with it. A malicious woman, the same as Margaret. A pity in many respects, as when she was younger she was much more agreeable.'

'We've met her husband,' Clare said. 'Did you ever?'

'As far as anyone was concerned it was just a tale put out by Gloria, indignant at being called an old maid.'

'He was real enough, even admitted that he had loved her deeply once.'

'And her?'

'Her love for him, we're not sure if it was real or feigned. Regardless, after three months of marriage, she took off and claimed more than her fair share of his assets.'

'She never loved anyone in this village, although there were a few men when she was younger. An emotionless woman apart from her prejudices. Never had a cat or a dog, and she used to complain if a dog barked. There is one family who is certain she poisoned theirs, a spaniel, noisy as all hell, but that's what you get in the country. Although not as bad as the noise from the Blatchfords with that old tractor of his.'

'Did she complain about it?'

'Gloria was at one end of the village, the Blatchfords down the other, but we could hear it clear enough.'

'Did you complain?'

'Not us, and besides, it didn't bother us much.'

One of the children wandered into the room. Tremayne and Clare left the house in a state of disrupted equilibrium. They did not expect their next visit, the manor house of Margaret Wilmot, to be any more pleasant.

Chapter 12

Rupert Baxter was in fine fettle, criticising Sheila Blatchford, when Tremayne and Clare entered his pub. Clare had to admit surprise as the woman had been his half-sister.

'One of your lunches,' Tremayne said as he sat on a stool at the bar. It was early afternoon, a time when the pub would normally have been three-quarters empty, but it was a full contingent that had greeted the two police officers.

Baxter was behind the bar, the Upminsters were sitting with Margaret Wilmot, as were the Fosters, the reason that Tremayne and Clare had not found her at her house. Woodcock's description of the condition of the building was an understatement. If, as Baxter had indicated, Hamish Foster was devoted to his wife, Tremayne thought the man would have better served her interests by removing her from the influence of malignant negativity.

'Fish pie, or a steak?' Baxter said.

'A steak for me, the pie for Yarwood.'

'Rough time at the Woodcocks'?' Baxter said.

'I thought it was confidential.'

'News travels fast.'

'Not from us, it doesn't.'

'Barry was on the phone to me, and Gwen had forewarned Margaret that you were on the way.'

'Why would she do that? There was no love lost between the two women.'

'There isn't, but Margaret is influential in this village. Some would say that she's too influential, but money speaks, and money commands respect, and she's got plenty of it. Anyone who gets on the wrong side of her soon feels her wrath.'

'Legal action?'

'That's about it. The Woodcocks are decent people, but they're not the sort of people to rock the boat. Gwen sucks up to Margaret, no option really, and Barry does what he's told. He could have made something of himself, but that's not him. Still, each to their own, that's what I say. In here, it's a no-man's land. It's where everyone chooses to not upset the others. Only with you and your sergeant here, tempers are starting to fray. Margaret even got upset with Eustace Upminster earlier, accused him of sitting on the fence.'

'Where she lives is not in good condition,' Clare said. Over in the corner, the woman in question was sipping her drink. She was casting dagger eyes at the two police officers.

'It must have been magnificent once, but now it's beyond repair,' Baxter said.

'Is it?'

'Margaret may tell you different, but it's old, rising damp, and it would need to be rebuilt from the ground up. Excessively expensive, and I doubt that Margaret could afford it. The National Trust were after it, an excellent example of a sixteenth-century manor house, but they shied away. One day, it'll collapse, and Margaret will be inside.'

'She may not be there.'

'It'll wait for her.'

'Haunted?'

'Supposedly,' Baxter said. 'There's one in the pub, an old man caught cheating at cards. They took him outside and beat him so bad he never recovered, but that was a few centuries ago.'

'You've seen him?' Clare asked. She was holding a glass of wine, drinking slowly as usual. Tremayne had a pint of beer, and slowly and beer didn't go together in the same sentence.

'Not me, although there are others who say they have. Anyway, he's benevolent, causes no trouble, not like some others in the village.'

'You were being vocal about Sheila Blatchford when we came in,' Tremayne said.

'Probably more than I should have been. A mouthy woman, even if we shared some parental DNA. I don't remember my father saying a bad word about anyone.'

'But you do, and Sheila did.'

'Mine's just sounding off. Sheila would take it to the next level, make it personal.'

'Barry and Gwen Woodcock have motives for the murders,' Clare said.

'Maybe they do, but I don't see it,' Baxter said. Two meals came through the hatch. Baxter placed them on the bar with some cutlery, as well as the salt and pepper.

'Why not?' Tremayne said. On his fork, a piece of meat.

'Sure, Barry's got the strength, and both have enough reason to hate Gloria and then Sheila and those remaining, but they've always gone with the flow. I saw Barry get upset once after a car had sped through the village, hit one of his cows, but apart from that, he'll not lose his temper. And as for Gwen, placid, earthy woman. Devoted to her children and Barry, even after what they said about him and James.'

'One question no one answers.'

'The one question no one knows the full truth about. James told me it was scurrilous what was said, an attempt to remove him from the pulpit, to bring in someone more to their liking.'

'The Reverend Tichborne?'

'He was put in the church by the bishop in Salisbury, no doubt to spite those that were trying to hijack the local church for their own purposes. Tichborne's not a bad man. He's more placid than James was, but even he is not going to take a hard-line ecclesiastical view of how the church services should be conducted, nor what they should do with sinners.'

'Such as?'

'Not burning in the village square or in hell. Gloria wanted those who did not profess piety to be ostracised from village life, me, for instance.'

'How did she intend that to happen?'

'It doesn't matter how she intended it. She wasn't going to achieve it, but she could certainly talk about it enough.'

'Bert and Sheila Blatchford?'

'Simple souls. Bert wasn't too bright, and Sheila probably didn't deserve what happened to her. Believe me, Margaret's next. Not because she's the natural successor, but because of the misery she exudes, the hold she has over people.'

'The same people who killed the other three?'

'Who knows? The quiet village, a haven of tranquillity and love. That's what they always try to convince you of, but the reality is the opposite.'

'Yours is not the first village we've investigated murders in,' Tremayne said.

***

Clare left Tremayne and Baxter and walked over to where Margaret Wilmot held court. The woman looked up, nodded for her to take a seat. Regardless, Clare had intended to anyway.

'Come to gloat over Sheila, have you?' Margaret said. Clare looked at the woman's face. She could see a hardness that had not been there before.

'I've come to solve three murders,' Clare said. She judged that a rebuke to the woman's previous comment would have amounted to nothing. Margaret Wilmot was clearly a person who formed her own opinions of people and events to the exclusion of facts.

'I'm next, you know,' Margaret said matter-of-factly, as if it did not concern her.

'Does this mean your group here are all threatened?'

'No. Desdemona's weak, and Hamish is not convinced of what we stand for. He'd rather have a pint of beer and his wife at home slaving for him, but she's here with us. And Eustace will look after Gladys, even if he's not too keen on her.'

'We've been with the Woodcocks.'

'Don't go thinking that they are going to get their farm when I die. I've seen to that.'

'You're a hard woman,' Clare said. 'We went up to your house. It's not in good condition, is it?'

'It will be.'

'When?'

'Once I've sold off some of my holdings in the village. Although I might not live long enough. Do you believe that Barry and Gwen Woodcock are innocent?'

'We're police officers. We deal in facts.'

The Upminsters sat still. Desdemona Foster had her head in her hands. Clare could see a weak woman who somehow controlled a strong man. Hamish Foster had pulled back from the group. According to all the information so far received, Hamish was a decent man who had no disputes with anyone in the village, and was regarded as congenial and down-to-earth.

'Barry Woodcock has sinned. He is beneath contempt,' Margaret Wilmot said.

'Regardless of what happened in the past, in this country a person is innocent until proven guilty. The Woodcocks are worried that you'll take their farm at some time.'

'My farm, I've given them six months to vacate or I'll have them evicted. Did they tell you that?'

'No. Should they have?'

'They killed the others, and now they're after me.'

Clare could see inconsistencies. However, she couldn't see any flaws in what the woman was saying, and if, as had been stated, the Woodcocks were being evicted, then why had they not mentioned it. Someone wasn't telling the truth, and dislikeable as the woman was, Margaret Wilmot was nobody's fool. She would have employed a lawyer to deal with her legal affairs, the

Woodcocks probably hadn't, or possibly didn't understand the consequences of what was to occur.

'I believe that you and your group's harassing of James Baxter led to his death, and that Barry Woodcock has been lambasted for no other reason than a group of men-haters decided that the two men were not worthy, or maybe they rejected you and Gloria, possibly even Sheila.'

Over at the bar Tremayne drank his beer, his ears pricked, waiting for someone to say something.

'I didn't hate men, nor did Gloria,' Margaret said.

'Nor do I,' Desdemona said, the first words she had said. Her husband leant over and put his arm around her.

'I think you've gone a little too far, Sergeant,' Hamish Foster said.

'Not far enough. Someone took a chainsaw from the Woodcocks. We've got our crime scene team down there looking for proof of who it was. Does anyone here want to own up to the crime, throw themselves on the mercy of the court, turn Queen's evidence, implicate one of the others?'

'My wife is not involved.'

'She wouldn't have had the strength to lift or pull Gloria Wiggins close up to the pulley, and wielding a chainsaw and cutting through human flesh and bone requires strength and a strong constitution, and Desdemona doesn't possess either in great measure,' Clare said.

'She doesn't, although I do. Are you about to accuse me?' Hamish Foster said. 'You've insulted Margaret, derided my wife as a weak woman, and devalued the good name of Gloria Wiggins.'

'You've not mentioned Bert and Sheila Blatchford,' Clare said.

'I will defend them if I must.'

'Hamish is a good man,' Margaret Wilmot said.

'We've never doubted that, but why does he sit here with you now, and before that, Sheila.'

'He's here because of me,' Desdemona said.

Chapter 13

Bemerton Road Police Station was hectic, with Superintendent Moulton noticeable around the building in his drive for budgetary control, a new set of key performance indicators to follow up on, a need to ensure that all reports were in and on time. The bane of the man's existence, Detective Inspector Keith Tremayne, sat back on his chair in his small office. The investigation into the murders out at Compton was at a crossroads. The necessary interviews had been conducted, but none too revealing in themselves. And then the crime scene investigators had been at every murder site, every place of interest, and had not found much, apart from proof that the person who had murdered Gloria Wiggins had been of sufficient physical strength to lift the woman free of the ground, and that Bert Blatchford's knife wounds were either frenzied or hurried, or possibly both.

The murder of Sheila, Bert's wife, was more perplexing. Pathology had confirmed that she had been dead before being sliced up with a chainsaw, the work so expertly done that parts of her could have been wrapped in plastic and sold at the supermarket in Salisbury as prime cuts of meat. It was clear that she had died in the barn where she had been found. The quantity of blood confirmed that death and dissection had occurred within five minutes of each other, and that the murderer would have been covered in as much blood as the chainsaw. That person's clothes had been found jammed in a crevice between two bales of hay nearby. Forensics had confirmed that they were overalls, not untypical in a farming community, and that the wearer had been a person of average height, and not overweight. The one unknown was how the murderer had removed the overalls, cleaned themselves up, and then left the farm. The noise of the chainsaw was not a significant consideration, as the murder had occurred during the hours when there would have been tractors in the fields and vehicles on the road, and the noise of the saw would not have necessarily warranted concern.

Clare focussed on her report, Tremayne longed for a cigarette. As he raised himself from his chair to go outside the building to light up, Superintendent Moulton came in.

'They're piling up again,' Moulton said. An uneasy truce existed between the degree-educated superintendent and his most experienced police officer. No mention had been made of Tremayne's enforced retirement for two months, a relief for him, a matter of concern for Moulton.

'I'll agree that it's a puzzle. No obvious clues, no evidence that points in one direction or the other,' Tremayne said. While the superintendent's efforts to make him retire had been annoying, Tremayne had to admit that the senior officer was a decent man, and a begrudging acceptance, almost a friendship, existed between the two men.

Moulton left as there was no more to be gained from his detective inspector, knowing full well that the man was the best he had, and he had no further input into the case that would help.

Outside the building, Tremayne lit his cigarette. Clare stood close by. 'We're not getting anywhere on the latest murders,' she said.

Tremayne could only agree. Three deaths, no concrete evidence, and a fractious community which appeared to say one thing and do another.

As much as Tremayne and Clare did not want to admit it, the most likely culprits were still the Woodcocks: the benign Barry, the earthy Gwen.

'Nothing from Jim Hughes and Pathology,' Tremayne said. The lack of evidence was disturbing. Amateurs invariably make a mistake, leave a clear sign as to whether the murderer was male or female, tall or short, right- or left-handed. The consensus with the chainsaw was that the person had been right-handed, an observation from Pathology based on the direction of the cutting action.

For once, Clare enjoyed the benefit of an early night at her cottage in Stratford sub Castle, her cat sitting on one side of her as she read a book, although not focussing on it as she should. Her life was troubled for two reasons: the murders in Compton, and the boyfriend, the good and decent Doctor Warner.

She did not sleep well that night, so much so that Tremayne felt the need to comment on her appearance the following day. For him, he had slept well, Jean by his side.

'What's for today?' Clare asked. It was still early in the office, and whereas many of the administrative staff were not in the police station, Tremayne and Clare were. They had established a routine of long hours during a murder investigation, not so long when there was not a case, although that was rare. A two-week break before the current murders had allowed Tremayne and Jean to head off down to Cornwall for a short break, and for Clare to visit her parents in Norfolk, with the usual probing into her personal life by her mother, the attempt by her father to defuse her mother's prying. Three days had been long enough in Norfolk, and since then Clare had been in the office on a daily basis, dealing with reports and studying for promotion.

Tremayne, a man who did not like being in his office, with a laptop before him that required attention, attention he did not want to give, raised himself from his seat. 'Back to the scene of the crimes,' he said.

Clare closed the lid of her laptop, grabbed her handbag and followed; the first stop, just outside the building, for Tremayne to take a few puffs of a cigarette before he settled himself into the passenger seat of his sergeant's car.

'Any ideas what to do first?' Clare said.

'Stephanie Underwood. She found the body, and so far she's the only half-sane person we've met.'

'Is she? She's hardly left the village in years.'

'A gossip, I'll grant you that, and maybe she's a little strange, but she has no perceivable motive.'

'Neither does Margaret Wilmot, but we're suspicious of her,' Clare reminded her senior, whose breath still reeked of stale cigarette smoke. She turned the fan of the car's heater to high to dissipate the smell and opened the top of her window a little. Outside the weather was chilly, but the occasional blast of cold air to her right was preferable to the smell in the car.

'The Wilmot woman's unpleasant and there are more than one or two who don't like her. Maybe Gloria Wiggins was another person who didn't, or she could have had a hold over her. We'll not find out by sitting here.'

'I'm driving as fast as I can.'

'Well, drive faster, and you can wind up that window. If my cigarette smoke disturbs you, you just need to say so.'

'It does.'

'Stop at the next shop and I'll buy some mints. What with you and Jean, you'll both be the death of me, and then what will the two of you have to talk about?'

'We'll find something else,' Clare said.

'No doubt you will. But getting back to the matter in hand, I don't trust Margaret Wilmot, and Hamish Foster sits there and lets his wife, Desdemona, be controlled by whoever's in charge of the group in the corner of the pub.'

'Unusual. Any other man would have ensured his wife did not come under negative influences.'

'He could be a closet fire and brimstoner,' Tremayne said.

'Do you still want to talk to Stephanie Underwood first?'

'Swing by her cottage. If she's there, we'll talk to her. Otherwise we'll pay the Fosters a visit.'

On entering the village, Clare turned to the right at the first road and drove up the slight incline and parked outside the neat and tidy cottage. In the house, a light burnt. Clare sensed that something was not right. She switched off the engine, removed the key and hurried up the path to the front door; it was ajar. She suppressed the desire to shout out and adopted a defensive mode as she pushed the door to open it further. Thankfully it did not creak on its hinges. Tremayne, not far behind Clare, moved to the rear of the house, signalling to his sergeant to be careful, and that he would come into the cottage from another direction.

Clare eased forward. The cottage was quiet, save for a television, the woman's lifeline to the outside world, blaring in the main room. Clare looked through a crack in the door. She could see the television screen, and the back of Stephanie Underwood's head. Clare relaxed at the sight of her, just before a heavy blow landed on the back of her head. She collapsed onto the hall floor, the noise sufficient to prompt Tremayne to move forward to assist her; the back door of the cottage had been open, allowing him to enter.

'Yarwood,' Tremayne said as he knelt down beside her. He had his phone in one hand, on speed dial for police backup and for the Emergency Services.

'What happened?' Clare said. She looked around her, not sure for one moment of her bearings.

'Someone hit you hard.'

'Did you see who?'

'I was in the kitchen. All I saw was a figure rushing out. I would have taken chase, but you were out for the count.'

'I'll be alright. Miss Underwood?'

'No need worrying about her.'

'Dead?'

'I've only looked briefly. Someone came in as she was watching the television, garrotted her with an electric cable. It's not a pretty sight.'

Clare slowly rose from her crouched position as a medic came in. She took over from Tremayne who had been struggling to lift his sergeant. His knees hurting from kneeling, another sign that he was getting older, but he didn't want to admit to it.

'She'll be fine,' the medic, a fresh-faced woman in her mid-thirties, said. 'We'll take her to the hospital just in case of concussion, delayed shock.'

'No, you won't,' Clare said. 'Just put on a bandage, give me an injection or whatever. We've got a killer on the loose. I'm needed here.'

'You'll be wasting your time arguing with Sergeant Yarwood,' Tremayne said.

'Suit yourself, but I'll need a signature that the young woman is not following medical advice,' the medic said.

'Whatever you want,' Clare said. 'There's another woman in the other room. According to Inspector Tremayne, she's dead, but you'd better check.'

The medic entered the room, took one look and came back. She was ashen-faced. 'I've seen enough dead bodies in my time, but not one that's been murdered.'

'It's always a bit of a shock the first time,' Tremayne said. 'The crime scene investigators will be here soon. You'll need to stay till they arrive, so they can take your finger and shoe prints.'

'Fine by me, although I'll wait outside.'

Two police officers arrived in uniform. 'We're establishing the crime scene,' one of them, a tall long-faced man with a Yorkshire accent, said. 'Anything else?'

'We need the roads in and out of the village sealed.'

'We've already started on that. There are only two roads anyway.'

'Do you reckon that someone's made it out?' Clare said to Tremayne.

'They've probably had time to leave. It's a long shot, but my money's on someone in the village. We need to interview as many as possible, and as soon as we can.'

'I'll get onto it,' Clare said. She did not feel well and her head throbbed. She knew that the medic had been correct and that she needed a day in a hospital bed, just in case, but now was not the time. The assumption that the murderer or murderers were focussing on the fire and brimstoners was dashed with the death of Stephanie Underwood. The woman was definitely not a zealot, and apart from her idiosyncrasies, there seemed to be no reason for her to have been murdered. But whatever the reason was, it possibly had a bearing on the other deaths in the village.

Jim Hughes and the crime scene team arrived. Hughes took one look at the body, and came back to where Clare was sitting, no longer on the floor, but on a chair that Tremayne had brought in from the kitchen. Tremayne had already left and had moved down to the pub. Interviews needed to be conducted, and people were required to account for their movements.

'One to two hours,' Hughes said.

'We've been here for nearly forty minutes, so whoever hit me is probably the murderer,' Clare said. She was feeling better for the rest and thanked the medic on the way out.

'Are you still going out with Doctor Warner?' the medic said.

'I'm not sure,' Clare said, knowing full well that she had said more than she should have. 'Personal, you'll understand,' she said by way of an aside, as she moved towards her car.

'Sorry, just making conversation. What I saw in there upset me.'

'Maybe you could do with the rest more than me.'

'You'll have a nasty bump, and a throbbing head. Do what you have to, and then go home. Give me a call, and I'll drop in later and check on you at home.'

'Is that what medics do?'

'No, but I don't live far from you, and I know where you live. Regardless, I'll give you a call later on to check. And no driving. Your inspector will have to drive for today.'

'Thanks. I'll tell him,' Clare said as she sat in her car.

'Sorry, you'll have to get someone else to drive, even now.'

'Fine. I can walk from here.'

The Reverend Tichborne appeared. 'Miss Underwood?' he said.

'She's been murdered,' Clare said. She had met the vicar on a couple of occasions and had not been impressed on either. To her, he was an unimposing figure, with a monotone voice that grated after only a short time.

'Is it possible to see her, say a prayer for her?'

'You can ask, but it's a crime scene. I'm afraid you'll have to say your prayer from the other side of the crime scene tapes. Afterwards, could you please come to the pub. We're interviewing everyone in the village. Whoever it was who did this, they were in the cottage when I was there.'

Clare left and walked down to the pub. It was only a five-minute walk, and the fresh air helped to clear her head. Inside the pub, a wood fire in one corner. Tremayne had set himself up in a small room off to one

side of the bar. The usual crowd were in the bar, even
though it was just after midday. No one looked shocked
or upset. Margaret Wilmot maintained her usual
impassive countenance, the Fosters looked as they always
did, the wife, Desdemona, in yet another summery dress,
this time a pattern of flowers in bloom on it, although
outside the pub was not the weather for flowers or
anything else much. Her husband, Hamish, sat by her
side. Gladys Upminster had her head down and did not
look happy, but that was not out of the ordinary for the
singularly despondent woman, Clare decided. Her
husband had a pint of beer in his hand.

Behind the counter in the bar, Rupert Baxter
stood. 'Fancy a drink, Sergeant Yarwood?' he called over
to Clare.

'I could do with something stiff, whisky under
normal circumstances, but for now, an orange juice.'

'Nasty bump on the head from what I hear,'
Baxter said. Regardless of the death of another villager, he
still maintained his cheerful demeanour.

'Someone in this pub more than likely gave it to
me,' Clare said loudly, looking for a reaction. She cast her
eyes around the pub, but nobody shifted uneasily in their
seat, no one averted their gaze.

Tremayne came out from where he had been
sitting. 'Send them in, Yarwood. One at a time and round
up those who are not here. Hughes is keeping me
updated from the woman's cottage. His team have found
some clues, especially relating to who hit you. Head
hurting?'

'Like hell,' Clare responded, which was true. The
fresh air outside had done some good, but inside the pub,
it was too hot. She felt her eyes wanting to close, her
mind wanting to shut down. She knew she should have

gone with the medic, but she knew her place: it was with Inspector Tremayne. Now was not the time to say she was too unwell to continue.

Chapter 14

Eustace Upminster was the first to be interviewed in the pub.

One of the uniforms came into the bar with the Reverend Tichborne. The uniform confided to Clare that the man had been a bit of a nuisance about wanting to see the dead body and to say a prayer.

Tichborne installed himself on a stool at the bar and ordered a rum. His hands were shaking, not unexpected under the circumstances. Murder, especially when it's someone you know, affects people in different ways. Some pretend to act normally, others act distraught and start crying for the dead person, eventually the crying turning to anger at the perpetrator.

Clare entered the room where Tremayne and Eustace Upminster sat.

'Nasty bump on the head,' Upminster said. He shifted uneasily on his seat. Clare had taken a few courses on body language, on how to interpret a person's actions.

She was putting them to use now, but Upminster wasn't giving much away.

'I'll be alright. My head's not the issue, is it? Who hit me on it is more relevant, who strangled Stephanie Underwood.'

Tremayne cleared his throat. 'We'll be recording this, is that acceptable?' he said to Upminster.

'Fine by me,' Upminster replied.

'Your name?'

'Eustace Upminster.'

'Stephanie Underwood's been murdered. No doubt everyone knows how and where.'

'Don't tell Rupert Baxter if you want to keep a secret, and besides, it's not unexpected.'

'What do you mean? Apart from being a gossip, the woman did not appear to have any particular views on anyone, and she was not one of Gloria Wiggins' group.'

'No, she wasn't, but she kept her ear to the ground. If anyone knew who had killed the three, it would be her.'

'Are you suggesting that she knew?'

'It's possible, although she may only have surmised it.'

'She never confided in us her suspicions,' Clare said.

'She was devoted to this village. I can't remember the last time that she wasn't here, and if she knew something, she wouldn't necessarily have told you.'

'What would she have done?'

'She would have let the village deal with it.'

'Taking the law into your own hands is a criminal offence.'

'Nothing as melodramatic as that. She would have adopted the view that these things sort themselves out in time.'

'Even if that meant more deaths?'

'Even. But that was Stephanie. A believer in fate, that's all. Not a bad way to live, saves all the hassle of worrying.'

'A bad way to die,' Clare said. She found Upminster's comments glib and inane. A woman had been murdered in her own home, watching her favourite programme on the television, yet Eustace Upminster was acting as if the woman had gone missing for a couple of hours.

Upminster left after a few more questions and Tremayne glanced down at the message on his phone. He dialled the sender.

'Yes, got it. Are you sure?' He ended the call, looked over at Clare. 'Get some juniors out here to take the statements. We've got a trip to meet up with someone.'

'I can't drive. The medic gave me some medicine, and besides, I'm not feeling so good.'

'I'll go on my own if you're not up to it,' Tremayne said.

'I'll sleep, you can drive. I can rest later, but today's important. I'm with you.'

***

Cuthbert Wiggins sat forlornly in the interview room at the police station close to his bank. He was not a happy man.

'He came quietly as a lamb,' the young sergeant at the station said.

'Any charges?' Tremayne asked. It had been a ninety-minute drive, and Clare had dozed most of the way. She felt better but not by a lot.

'We've cautioned him. We thought you'd want to deal with the charging. Nasty bump on your head,' the sergeant said. Clare had heard the comment a few too many times now, and it was starting to wear thin.

Tremayne took hold of a coffee that the station sergeant gave him; Clare kept to a glass of water. She realised that she was close to passing out. She excused herself and headed to the ladies' toilet. Inside, she splashed water on her face and steadied herself against the wall. She took a deep breath, went out and resumed her position alongside Tremayne. The two of them entered the interview room. A uniform stood to one side.

'Sorry about this,' Wiggins said.

'We'll follow this by the book, Mr Wiggins,' Tremayne said. He cautioned the man again and followed the correct procedure. Cuthbert Wiggins was no longer a person of interest; now he was intimately involved after Jim Hughes had found damning evidence against the man.

'Mr Wiggins, we have incontrovertible evidence that you were in Stephanie Underwood's cottage at the time of her death,' Tremayne said.

'I know it looks bad for me,' Wiggins replied, 'but she was dead when I arrived. I found her there, dead, still warm.'

'You'll not make a criminal if what you're saying is true. They found a monogrammed handkerchief, your initials.'

'My wife gave me a dozen for my last birthday. She likes to do things like that.'

'You dropped it.'

'I took it out when I was checking the woman.'

'The full story,' Clare said.

'Very well,' Wiggins said. 'I told you before that Gloria took plenty of my assets when we divorced.'

'You did.'

'When we first married, we drew up wills naming each other the beneficiary in the event of our deaths. I've changed mine obviously to my current wife's name. Gloria, I have since found out, did not, or if she had, she had not registered the will. If that is correct, then I am the beneficiary of her estate, the cottage and any money she may have had.'

'Why Stephanie Underwood?'

'It seemed a good idea at the time. Gloria hadn't registered a subsequent will, but she may have written another. I needed to know, and I didn't want to wait, and I thought Gloria's next-door neighbour might have known something.'

'Why would she?' Tremayne said.

'I don't know. It was just a hunch, but if there were money that I could claim, then I would. In her death, there may have been some redemption for what she did. I drove there, parked some distance from the village and walked through the fields and up to the back of the cottage. No one saw me, and apart from that handkerchief, you wouldn't have known that I'd been there.'

'We would have. There are fingerprints in the cottage, no doubt yours when we check. Also, a walking stick, the end of which you had held when you hit Sergeant Yarwood over the head.'

'I panicked. I wouldn't hurt a fly, but I knew that if I had been seen there, I would be charged with murder.'

'Mr Wiggins, you may be a fool, and you may have hit me, but you're not a murderer,' Clare said. 'There has been another person in that cottage, and there is evidence that that person strangled Stephanie Underwood.'

'She looked so peaceful there. I sat with her for a while.'

'Why?'

'It just seemed the right thing to do. Nobody should die like that.'

'You didn't care when Gloria died.'

'Not as much as I should, but the next-door neighbour deserved better.'

'Had you met her before?'

'No. I saw her that one time I came to the village, but it was many years ago, and she never saw me. Gloria said who she was.'

'How did you get into the cottage?' Clare asked.

'The door was open. I found her sitting there, a cable around her neck. That's the truth, and I'm sorry, Sergeant. I panicked.'

'Mr Wiggins, you've committed a crime. You'll be charged with assault and leaving the scene of a crime.'

'My wife will worry if I'm not at home tonight.'

'You'll be allowed to phone her to let her know. For tonight, you'll be held at the police station. Tomorrow, you can apply for bail.'

'Even from the grave Gloria causes trouble. I only wanted what was mine, and I'm sorry the next-door neighbour is dead.'

'So am I,' Clare said.

Tremayne drove back to Clare's cottage, Jean was at the door on their arrival. 'I'm staying the night,' she said to Clare. 'You need someone to fuss over you.

115

Tremayne told me what happened. It must have come as a big shock.'

'It did,' Clare said, although all she wanted to do was to go to bed and sleep.

Chapter 15

Tremayne, on his own for once, forsook the opportunity to have a few drinks at his local pub, and returned to Bemerton Road Police Station. On his arrival, he made for his office by way of Superintendent Moulton's. Tremayne knew the man would be interested in how the murder investigation was progressing, and Clare's well-being after she'd been hit on the head.

In Moulton's office, Tremayne updated his senior, even having a cup of coffee with him. This time no mention was made of retirement, or how long it would take to solve the case.

Tremayne left Moulton's office, and walked down the two flights of stairs to his own office. Waiting for him were two officers, both sergeants. Kyle Sutherland, degree-educated, ambitious, the taller of the two and very capable, had been looking for a berth in Homicide for some time. The only problem for Tremayne was that Sutherland was full-on, with no perceptible sense of humour, a man who ran marathons for the fun of it.

Tremayne knew Sutherland would irritate him, and besides he was soon to be an inspector and he'd want to be the senior investigating officer in Homicide. As far as Tremayne was concerned, the job was Clare's when he decided to retire.

The second of those waiting in his office, Danny Woo, was older than Sutherland and more experienced. Tremayne liked him, although the man eschewed any further attempts at gaining professional qualifications. Clare had the necessary degree, so did the marathon runner, but Woo, Chinese but born in England, did not. And as he had freely admitted to Tremayne, he was content to remain a sergeant, and his life was okay. A small house in the country, a wife, two children, and a cat were all he wanted. Tremayne had to agree with the man, as he had had the opportunity to become a chief inspector on more than one occasion but he had never pushed for it. There was always another murder to solve, another pub for a drink, and the higher echelons of the police force demanded more responsibility, setting an example, and neither had appealed.

Danny Woo stood as Tremayne entered his office; Sutherland remained sitting, a sign of arrogance, Tremayne thought. Deference to a superior, even if not a requirement, always showed a mark of respect; Sutherland not willing to grant that.

'You both stayed out at Compton and interviewed those in the pub,' Tremayne said. 'Any inconsistencies, anything untoward?'

'Our reports have been sent, full transcripts as well as the audio recordings,' Sutherland said in a tone of indifference.

'I'm sure they're thorough. Just give me your impressions of the people, their body language.'

118

'Could we get an update from you first?' Danny Woo asked.

'Sure. We've charged Cuthbert Wiggins with hitting Sergeant Yarwood. He admitted to that crime, and Yarwood is going to be fine. She's tough and she will be in the office tomorrow. Wiggins claims that he entered Stephanie Underwood's house purely because he wanted to see what she knew about any later wills that Gloria Wiggins may have written. He stated that he found Miss Underwood dead, and that he panicked when Yarwood entered the cottage. That's when he hit her. He then fled across the fields, avoiding me and anyone else in the village.'

'He was seen,' Sutherland said.

'Wiggins did not murder Stephanie Underwood,' Tremayne continued. 'Jim Hughes and his crime scene investigators found evidence of another person. Just a smudged fingerprint on a door handle, and evidence that someone had scuffed a wooden floor with a muddied boot. It looks as if the murderer was a man, but it's not certain.'

'And Wiggins?' Woo asked.

'He'll probably be bailed tomorrow. No doubt his bank will suspend him, but he did not murder the woman, and unless we come up with something conclusive, he did not kill Gloria Wiggins either.'

'Very well,' Sutherland said. 'Sergeant Woo and I conducted our interviews. The only alibis from anyone that we spoke to are not irrefutable, purely each corroborating the other as to where they were. Barry and Gwen Woodcock were at their farm, not proof in itself. The Fosters, Hamish and Desdemona, were at home, as was Margaret Wilmot. Eustace and Gladys Upminster were tucked up in bed, according to them, although Gladys was crying most of the time during the interview.'

'She has some psychological issues,' Tremayne admitted.

'So we gathered from your and Sergeant Yarwood's reports,' Sutherland said.

'The Reverend Tichborne?'

'At the rectory. A strange man, he kept quoting parables, but nothing untoward. Supposedly he was a nuisance at the crime scene.'

'He wanted to get close to the body, say a prayer. He wasn't allowed, and he got angry. How about Rupert Baxter?'

'He claims that he was upstairs in the pub,' Woo said.

'Claims?' Tremayne said.

'That's in our report,' Sutherland said.

'Okay, remiss of me for not reading it, but I want your impressions, not written words.'

'Outside of the pub, it was a couple of hours later, Barry Woodcock came up to us. He was with his wife, Gwen.'

'And?'

'According to them, and they were anxious not to be seen to be telling tales or casting slurs, but they said that Rupert Baxter was with Margaret Wilmot, tucked up together at her manor house.'

'What!' Tremayne exclaimed, almost jumping out of his seat at the news.

'An unusual pair,' Sutherland said. 'Baxter's a jovial, easy-going man. Margaret Wilmot is not. Rather severe in her manner, and definitely not a woman to be trifled with. She was tough in the interview, answered what was asked, said no more. Emotionless.'

'Those two bring an unknown into the investigation. You've not quizzed either of them about this disparity?'

'We conducted the interviews as required,' Woo said. 'And besides, you and Yarwood have a closer understanding of the village of Compton and its occupants. We believed we were correct in leaving it to you and Sergeant Yarwood to follow up.'

'Great job, and yes, you're correct. Although why the Woodcocks never told us about Margaret Wilmot and Rupert Baxter before is of concern, and if the two young lovers are involved, how does this impact on the investigation?' Tremayne said.

'Young?' Sutherland said.

'Maybe not so young, but they've kept their distance before, and now we are informed that they may be cavorting up there in the manor house. The problem is that everyone protects everyone else, and it's almost impossible to find the truth. And what is it with Tichborne? We've never heard him reciting passages from the Bible before.'

'Not so many parables, but he mentioned Lazarus rising. Does it mean anything to you?'

'It's an oblique reference to Margaret Wilmot.'

***

Clare slept well that night. The medic came over at one stage to the cottage, although by then Clare was upstairs, so she spent an hour with Jean, chatting and drinking tea. The next morning, Clare enjoyed a home-cooked English breakfast: bacon, eggs, sausages, and toast. Tremayne, left to himself, managed to pour cornflakes into a bowl and add milk.

In Compton a light mist had settled over the place, as if a forewarning of doom. Clare liked Stratford sub Castle where her cottage was, but Compton left her cold. Even on a bright day it had little charm, but with a mist, it looked eerie and unloved.

The Woodcocks had made the aspersion about Margaret Wilmot and Rupert Baxter. They would be the first to interview. After that, a visit to the manor house.

Tremayne thought that Barry and Gwen were stupid or naïve, or they were playing a game where not only their fingers would get burnt.

Gwen opened the door on their arrival, her expression clearly saying that they weren't welcome. 'Come in if you must,' she said. She was wearing a blouse and a skirt, tidy for her as she was not a woman to dress up, not even for the pub. She still wore no makeup, and Clare could see that her attempt at brushing her hair had left her with a somewhat wild look.

Tremayne took a seat in the kitchen. Welcome or not, there were questions to answer, proof to be given. 'We've received an update from Sergeants Woo and Sutherland,' he said.

A pregnant pause while no one spoke. Eventually, 'What we said about Margaret and Rupert, is that it?'

'We need the truth,' Clare said. Apart from a slight headache, she was back to normal.

'We don't lie,' Gwen said.

'We need to know why you have decided to reveal it now, and what proof do you have?'

'Barry will be back soon. He'll be able to answer for both of us.'

'You and your husband have a habit of not telling the truth,' Tremayne said. He fixed the woman with a steely look, not sure what to make of her.

'We don't indulge in gossip.'

'And Margaret Wilmot and Rupert Baxter are not gossip?'

'It seemed appropriate to mention it to the other two. I saw them up at her house, very friendly they were. She was even smiling.'

'That doesn't mean they were involved.'

'It does to Barry and me. Margaret doesn't smile that much, and with Rupert, she was like a little child. I could see them holding hands. I knew what was going on.'

Barry Woodcock came into the house. 'I saw your car pull in.'

'You took your time coming,' Tremayne said. There was no friendliness in his voice.

'I was ploughing the field over the other side of the farm. Once you start, you've got to finish.'

Tremayne wasn't sure if it was a satisfactory answer but did not comment.

'You and your wife felt the need to inform Sergeants Woo and Sutherland that Margaret Wilmot and Rupert Baxter are romantically involved,' Clare said.

'It's none of our business, but it's true.'

'Because your wife says so?'

'If my wife believes it, then so do I.'

Clare looked over at Tremayne and could see that he was ready to move on. There were chains to rattle, people to put on edge, tempers to raise, and above all mistakes for the villagers to make. Both police officers could tell that the place was incestuous, not necessarily in the biblical sense, although Rupert Baxter and Sheila Blatchford had shared a father, but in the behaviour of all concerned.

Outside the farmhouse, Tremayne lit up a cigarette and let out a sigh of exasperation. 'The two of them are enough to drive anyone crazy. And as for Barry Woodcock's denial about his involvement with James Baxter, I'm not so sure it was as innocent as he proclaims.'

'It was Margaret Wilmot who said she saw them that time, and then Gloria Wiggins who damned them in the church. Why do the Woodcocks keep quiet on all they know?'

'There's more, but first we'll talk to Rupert Baxter. If he denies it, then we'll go and see Margaret Wilmot.'

'We're going to see her anyway,' Clare said.

'You're right. Into the hornet's nest.'

'The manor house?'

'You're driving.'

Chapter 16

'What is it with this village?' Tremayne said as Clare parked close to the front door of the manor house. Both Margaret Wilmot and Rupert Baxter were waiting for them.

'It looks as if we're about to find out,' Clare said. The sight of the two people at the front of the house was unexpected.

'You're wrong,' Margaret said as Tremayne went to shake her hand. She was wrapped in a heavy coat; Baxter wore only a light jacket.

'Wrong about what?'

'That we murdered the others to prevent them talking.'

'How did you know we were coming up here?' Tremayne said. He had a packet of cigarettes in his hand.

'Barry Woodcock phoned.'

'Why is another question, but Baxter, how did you get here so quick? The Woodcocks' farm is closer than your pub, and Yarwood's not a slow driver.'

'I was already here.'

'Which means?'

'It means nothing.'

'So why did Woodcock phone you?' Tremayne said, directing his question at Margaret.

'He told me that you'd been sniffing around his place again, annoying Gwen.'

'You're evicting the Woodcocks, and they make a damning indictment that you and Baxter are carrying on a clandestine affair, and then Barry phones you up to tell you what he's done and that we're on our way.'

'He didn't tell us of his accusation. However, he did tell us you were on the way.'

'It's true, this affair?'

'It's not clandestine. The fact that we choose not to broadcast the fact does not make it illegal or immoral. We're both single, over the age of consent, and it's our business, not yours or anyone else's in this village.'

'You're the purveyor of decency and morality. Hardly the actions of a devout woman,' Tremayne said.

'I'm still a woman. Rupert's a sinner, but he's a decent man, and he told you nothing, nor did anyone else who knows.'

'Who else knows?'

'It's not a subject for general conversation.'

'The Woodcocks? Why would they tell us about you two, and then forewarn you?'

'Gwen may have seen us, but neither of them is too bright, and as to why, then you'd better ask them.'

'What will you do?' Clare asked.

'The Woodcocks will need to tell me why,' Margaret Wilmot said.

'No more than that?'

'No. The Wilmots and the Woodcocks have a shared history. No doubt some interbreeding, so I wouldn't be surprised if there's a shared ancestor between us. I'll evict them if I must, but I'll not throw them to the wolves.'

'That makes no sense,' Tremayne said.

'They will feel the full force of the Wilmot anger, but they will remain unscathed. A frank and honest admission of what they've done may go in their favour.'

'What does that mean?'

'Loyalty and honesty are two virtues that reap rewards. If they admit to what they've done, then I will reconsider their eviction.'

'Why?'

'It would be charitable, and Rupert and I are beyond concealing the truth. He's asked me to marry him. I don't know why as I am a dragon, and I'll make his life hell.'

'Will you?' Clare asked.

'I will, although I'll not live in that pub, and he won't live here.'

'We'll argue, I know that,' Baxter said, 'but with Margaret, life will be interesting.'

Tremayne and Clare saw the two most unlikely lovebirds briefly touch hands. Clare thought it romantic; Tremayne thought it was too daft to contemplate.

***

Little was said on the drive back into Salisbury, as the conversation at Margaret Wilmot's house had left both Tremayne and Clare unsure of what it all meant. Back at the police station, Tremayne retreated to his office, Clare to her laptop. She entered the name Wilmot into Google

Search and pressed enter. A check of the land records stretching back at least five hundred years showed that the Wilmots had been the major landowners for most of that time. There was no mention of the Woodcocks, reflective of their lowly status.

Tremayne came out and sat next to Clare. 'Are you sure you're alright? You were out cold yesterday after Wiggins hit you on the head.'

'He's innocent of murder,' Clare said. 'And yes, I'm fine. Jean looked after me well.'

'Left me on my own. No doubt you were fed well.'

'Hungry?'

'Starving,' Tremayne said.

'Very well. I'm treating. The Pheasant Inn. You can have one of their lunches.'

'We'd do better out at Baxter's pub.'

'I'm not sure what to say after that revelation at the manor house.'

'Nor am I, but it's confirmed. We should find out who else knew and if it's a motive. And what about Tichborne and his mentioning Lazarus? The man rose from the dead, the same as Margaret. Was he trying to give Woo and Sutherland a lead?'

'Tichborne first, the lunch afterwards.'

'We can deal with both at the same time. Get Tichborne to meet us at the pub, twenty minutes. We'll use the backroom to interview him,' Tremayne said.

At the pub, the jovial host held sway. What had been said out at the Wilmots' ancestral home was not mentioned. Tremayne ordered a steak, Clare only a sandwich. Reverend Tichborne came in, ordered a small sherry and entered the backroom at Clare's beckoning. No one else was in the pub, other than Baxter.

'Reverend Tichborne, you mentioned Lazarus at the interview yesterday with Sergeants Woo and Sutherland. Why?'

'Did I?'

'You did. We have a recording of the interview. Is it because of Margaret Wilmot and her miraculous recovery?'

'It wasn't miraculous.'

'Then why Lazarus? No one else has returned from the dead, and Stephanie Underwood's not coming back, or do you believe she might? Are you a closet fire and brimstoner, the same as Margaret Wilmot, Sheila Blatchford, and Gloria Wiggins?'

'I believe in what is written, if that's what you mean?'

'A literal interpretation or a belief in the divine?'

'Those that died did so for a reason.'

'Is that a way of justifying your actions? Could you have killed them?'

'I'm a minister of the church.'

'That doesn't prove your innocence, Reverend.'

'I'm not sure what you mean,' Tichborne said. Clare could see that he was a nervous and fragile man as he sat in front of Tremayne.

'Okay, some starters. The truth about Margaret Wilmot,' Tremayne said. Clare knew that he was trying to get the vicar to reveal hidden unknowns. If Margaret and Rupert were involved, then what else was going on in the village, and was it relevant to the case? Four people had died so far, and yet there was no clear motive connecting them. Tremayne was pinning his hopes on the vicar, the one man in the village who had not been born there, not grown up there, not played hopscotch with the other

129

children, not gone to the same schools, dated and married each other.

'Margaret Wilmot is a wealthy woman, and she controls a lot of lives in this village.'

'Why?'

'That's the way it is.' Tichborne squirmed on his seat. Tremayne focussed more intensely, looking directly into the man's eyes, not blinking.

'What about Margaret? Men, boyfriends, lovers?'

'It's not my place to condemn a person.'

'Four of your parishioners, zealots or otherwise, have died, and you're sitting there telling us that it's not your place to condemn. Reverend Tichborne, it's up to you to clear up this sorry mess and to start telling us the truth. Once again. Margaret Wilmot, men, boyfriends, lovers?'

'Very well,' Tichborne said as he sat back on his seat resignedly. 'Margaret has a special relationship with Rupert Baxter.'

'At last, the truth.'

'You knew?'

'Not from you, and we only found out yesterday. What is it with these people? Don't they want to solve the murders, to prevent any more?'

'Are there going to be more?'

'Why not? Margaret Wilmot and Rupert Baxter are sleeping together. Is that true?'

'Yes.'

'And you, as a vicar, what do you think about it?'

'It is not for me to comment.'

'You're the vicar of the church, a man. You have a right to an opinion. Whether you voice it out loud or not is not the issue, but what is your view?'

'I counselled Margaret to exercise caution.'

'What's the truth with the Wilmots and the Woodcocks? Why do the Woodcocks hide what they know about Margaret and others, and then tell two police officers about the lovers up at the manor house?'

'It's complex.'

'Complex we can deal with. Concealment, we can't. Reverend Tichborne, the truth. What was the issue with Stephanie Underwood? Why were you so agitated at her cottage? Why the scene because they wouldn't let you in? And don't tell me that you were having an affair with her. We've had enough surprises as it is. Did you murder her? Did you want to say a prayer for her to atone for your sin?'

'No, yes. I'm confused.'

'Confused about what? Confused that you killed her, and now you can't remember why, or maybe you're not sorry for what you did.'

'She was going to say something.'

'What?'

'About me. It was too horrible, I couldn't let her.'

'What was she going to say?'

'She was going to tell the village that I killed my wife.'

'Did you?'

'It was an accident, but I told no one. Stephanie found out.'

'How?'

'I was standing next to my wife's grave. I loved her, but she used to have these periods when she'd accuse me of the most heinous things, things that no man should be accused of. If I spoke to another woman, even though she was a parishioner, my wife would become fiercely jealous, threaten to stick a knife into me during the night.'

131

'The view in the village is that your wife was a gentle kind soul.'

'She was, but behind closed doors, she could become violent. Well, sometimes it just became too much.'

'So what did you do?'

'My wife had tablets to calm her down. Most times she'd take them, but sometimes she wouldn't.'

'And?'

'I used to crush them and put them in a drink. One day, I gave her too many. It was an accident, I swear it. Her death was deemed as natural, purely because the tablets had diluted in her system, but I know it was because I had made an error. I've chastised myself since then, and I would stand by her grave and talk to her. I'm sure she heard and forgave me. Stephanie overheard me once. It was not long ago, and she was threatening to tell if I didn't stop the other killings.'

'Did she believe you were responsible?'

'She thought I was.'

'Why didn't you tell us this before?'

'Because I killed Gloria.'

'Rubbish. Who are you protecting?'

'Nobody, it's the truth.'

'Reverend Tichborne, you may be a good vicar, but you're a lousy liar. You could not have killed Gloria Wiggins. It would have required someone stronger than you to move her body out to the garage where she was strung up. Who are you protecting, and did Stephanie see you?'

'I deserve to be punished for what happened to my wife.'

'Did you kill Stephanie Underwood?'

'I saw her there, sitting in front of her television. I wanted to explain to her, but she was right. Why should I not be punished for my wife's death?'

'Reverend Tichborne, we've read the report into the death of your wife. You did not kill her, and there were no signs of any unusual levels of drugs in her body. You may blame yourself, but no court would convict you. No doubt there are those in the community here in Compton who would blame you, especially if Miss Underwood had said something, but it would be hearsay, nothing more. Did the woman deserve to die?'

'I couldn't help myself. She was sitting there, her back to me, and there was the cable on the ground. I picked it up and wrapped it around her neck. She barely moved.'

'And how did you feel afterwards?' Clare asked.

'Gratified. As though a burden had been lifted.'

'Yarwood, get a patrol car down here,' Tremayne said.

Tichborne offered no resistance as he was placed in handcuffs and taken out of the pub. On the street, a smattering of the locals stood, aghast at what had transpired.

On his return from the patrol car to the pub, Tremayne took hold of Baxter's collar. 'The next time you feel like telling the neighbourhood what is going on in your pub, you'll find yourself in a cell at Bemerton Road Police Station. Do I make myself clear?'

'You do,' Baxter said.

Chapter 17

Superintendent Moulton was delighted, so much so that he patted Tremayne on the back. Neither Tremayne nor Clare was pleased with what they had had to do, but the Reverend Tichborne had admitted his guilt. Forensics were checking the evidence from the murdered woman's cottage, and Tichborne had supplied a sample of DNA, as well as a description of what he had been wearing that night. Jim Hughes had sent out a team to the vicar's rectory to look for further evidence.

'That's still three more murders to solve,' Clare said after Moulton had left, and it was just the two of them in the office again.

Tremayne stood up and looked out of the window. 'Let's get out of here. I could do with a pint.'

Neither spoke much in the pub, not in Compton this time. Tremayne was seriously annoyed with Baxter for telling others what was going on. The wall between the back of the bar where Baxter stood and the room where they had conducted the interview was thin, and the conversation had obviously been heard. Even so, Baxter should have kept his mouth shut, and he was still a strong contender for a charge of murder.

The two officers called it an early night, and by seven in the evening, Clare was back in her cottage and Tremayne was back home in Wilton. Clare's head, though still a little sore, gave her no more cause for concern, and she went to bed early, hopeful of a peaceful night, knowing full well that out in Compton another murderer was still on the loose.

Tremayne phoned her up just as she was dropping off to sleep. 'We'll interview Tichborne tomorrow morning. He knows more than he's told us so far.'

Clare closed her eyes. Her cat slept at the bottom of the bed, but for her sleep came later. In her mind, all that had transpired so far in Compton: the murders, the people, the vicar's confession, and Cuthbert Wiggins, a man with a wife who had so far not been seen. Clare could see her as a possibility, especially if she was a jealous woman, as was Tichborne's wife supposedly. More research into that woman's death was needed, and if there was any doubt, then she would have to be exhumed. Finally, at eleven o'clock, Clare fell asleep. The alarm, the next thing she knew, rang at six in the morning.

Seven in the morning and Tremayne was already in the office when Clare arrived. She poured herself a coffee and went and sat with her senior. Downstairs, the Reverend Tichborne was enjoying his breakfast, better than the one that Clare had prepared for herself.

In Compton, another day dawned, the day when hopefully all the pieces would come together. If Margaret Wilmot and Rupert Baxter could keep a relationship, if

135

not entirely secret, then at least discreet, then what else lurked in that village?

At eight-thirty, the Reverend Tichborne was brought up to the interview room. He had a lawyer with him. Tremayne knew the man, Bob Exeter. Competent, decent, and a man who would not allow police badgering of his client.

The formalities completed, Tremayne led off with the questioning. 'Reverend Tichborne, what other secrets lie in the village of Compton?'

'I don't think I'll be a man of the cloth for much longer, do you?' Tichborne replied. He looked despondent and lost, a not unusual condition for a person after their first night behind bars.

'A man is innocent until proven guilty.'

'I am guilty. I've admitted to the crime.'

'We'll still want Forensics to confirm that you were in Stephanie Underwood's cottage. Honestly, you're not the person we expected to arrest for murder.'

'Murderers come in all shapes and sizes,' Tichborne said.

'They do. Moving on from that one murder, what do you know about the others?'

'Suspicions, that's all.'

'Whom do you suspect?'

'Rupert Baxter had a motive, the death of his brother. So did Barry Woodcock, and his wife will do anything to protect her man.'

'Protect him from what? Gloria and her cohorts were only casting aspersions. Not a crime in itself, although unpleasant to the person on the receiving end. Murder is criminal, and there's a prison sentence for the perpetrator. Would either man have risked that?'

'Rupert may have thought he was smart enough to get away with it, and Barry wouldn't have thought it through.'

'Admittedly, both could have killed all three, but Gwen could only have killed two of them.'

'Why?'

'Sheila Blatchford's body would have required a degree of aptitude, the physical strength to have wielded the chainsaw. It's unlikely that Gwen could have killed her.'

Bob Exeter, up until now quiet, felt the need to make a point. Tremayne knew him to be a taciturn man, not given to wild gestures or excessive speaking. His manner could be deceptive to those who didn't know him, but Tremayne knew he deserved respect.

'You made an earlier comment that you still needed to prove that my client, Reverend Tichborne, is guilty as charged. Why?' Exeter said.

Clare liked the look of the man: confident, no more than forty-five, and fit.

'We've got a confession, that's true,' Tremayne said, 'but Reverend Tichborne has already stated that he killed his wife when we know for a fact that he didn't.'

'And you think the confession that you have now may be false?'

'No. Our forensics and crime scene team are checking through the evidence, trying to ascertain the truth as to why he killed Stephanie Underwood.'

'I told you,' Tichborne said. 'She wanted to expose me as the murderer of my wife. I couldn't let her do that.'

'It makes no sense,' Tremayne said. 'You obviously had an issue with your wife's death, a morbid belief that somehow you had been responsible.'

137

'It's true. I was confused. I wanted to pay for what I had done to my wife. I wanted to remain and administer to my flock in Compton. Stephanie came between what I knew I should do and what I wanted.'

'I know we've been over this before, but why kill her? There's no record of her causing any harm in the village, and even if she had been a gossip, it was only harmless chattering, not the sort for people to take offence, and certainly not the sort to incite people to retribution and anger, even violence. Your position would have been safe, and no one would have believed her. You were a respected man in the community, a leader, yet you decided to take the life of a harmless old woman.'

'I told you. It was gratifying to kill her and to see her sitting there, peaceful and at ease.'

'I'll be requesting a psychiatric evaluation, Reverend Tichborne,' Tremayne said. 'Also, I'll make a request for your wife to be exhumed. The report stated death due to natural causes, but we'll let our pathologist check her out.'

'You'll find that it's true,' Tichborne said.

'Why didn't you admit to it at the time?'

'I wanted to, but I was afraid. I'm not a brave man, you must know that.'

'My client is innocent until proven guilty,' Exeter said.

'That's understood, but what we've heard from the mouth of your client is that not only is he guilty of one murder, he may now be guilty of two.'

'I'm guilty of one, don't you hear me,' Tichborne said, his voice animated, its pitch raised. 'My wife was an accident, although I blame myself. I was under stress from her complaining, and I didn't look at the dosage. It should have been two tablets crushed in her drink, but I put ten. Don't you hear me? Don't you believe me?'

Clare thought to call for a doctor as the man was frenzied and on his feet. Instead, she grabbed him by his right arm and put him back in his chair. Tichborne broke down, sobbing, his head on the table.

'You'll need to halt this interview,' Exeter said.

'Ten minutes,' Tremayne's reply. Tichborne was still not telling the truth, and the man had issues. He had killed Stephanie, there seemed to be no doubt on that, but the reason why still eluded them.

Ten minutes elapsed before the interview continued. Tichborne was once again stable.

'Reverend Tichborne, we can see that you are an emotional man, given to extremes. Is that a fair assumption?'

'It is.'

'Is it also possible that your confession of the murder of Stephanie Underwood is false?'

'I killed her. I deserve to be punished.'

Tremayne looked over at Exeter. The lawyer offered no reaction.

'The time between the woman's death and my arrival at the cottage was no more than sixty to ninety minutes,' Clare said.

'I saw you,' Tichborne said.

'From where?'

'I can see the cottage from the upstairs of the rectory.'

'Did you see another person at the cottage?'

'I saw a man. He left after you had entered.'

'Did you recognise him?'

'Not from that distance.'

'Then how did you know it was me?'

'Your car, the clothes you were wearing. But the man left soon after you arrived. He crouched behind a hedge on leaving the cottage, and then after a few minutes made his way up through the fields.'

'Did you see his car?'

'No. He would have parked on a back road behind some trees. I can't see that far, and I can't see the road out of the village. That's the truth.'

'Why did you make a scene with wanting to see the dead woman? A sense of duty, a ghoulish attraction?'

Tremayne wrapped up the interview after a succession of vague answers. He could see that it was going around in circles. The Reverend Tichborne, if he was psychiatrically disturbed by the events surrounding his wife's death, Tremayne knew, then he would be found not guilty of the murder of Stephanie Underwood due to diminished responsibility.

***

Two things happened in Compton. The first and the most significant was that the opposing groups came together. On one side, Rupert Baxter and his liberal view of the world. On the other, Margaret Wilmot, now a known lover of Rupert. Eustace Upminster and Hamish Foster vacillated between the two groups; ideologically more in Rupert's corner, committed through marriage to the other. Barry and Gwen Woodcock kept neutral. The setting was the pub, not the church.

The second thing to happen was that a committee of the church elite was in the village and at the church. They had been met and informed by the crime scene team and the uniforms on duty that even the bishop himself couldn't get them permission to enter the rectory.

One of the three churchmen phoned Tremayne and received a similar response. If they wanted to see Tichborne, then Bemerton Road was where they needed to be, and subject to only one of them entering the cell, then Tremayne would permit it.

The three left, having driven past the pub on the way into the village and on the way out, not realising that some of the answers were in there.

'Tichborne was always an odd character,' Baxter said. He stood behind the bar dispensing drinks. A time of unity did not prevent him from profiting as he accepted payment for the drinks that everyone seemed to want. Margaret held a gin and tonic, Rupert a pint of beer.

'Fitted right in,' Eustace Upminster said.

'What do you mean?' Barry Woodcock said, his wife holding his arm. Her man was in the lion's den, and she was there to protect him.

'It's just an observation. Not all of us like each other, but we maintain a united front against outsiders.'

'It's our village,' Margaret said.

'Why murder Stephanie?' Eustace said. 'She was a busybody, but she's not the only one in this village. Margaret's quick with a scurrilous comment, and Gloria could dish the dirt as good as anybody, and from what we've heard, she had a few skeletons in the cupboard.'

'The mysterious husband?' Rupert said.

'It was him that hit Sergeant Yarwood on the head. They arrested him for it.'

'But what did he want?'

'The police have kept that under wraps, but we can surmise. Gloria, how much money did she have? Margaret, you're the one who understands such things. What do you reckon?'

'The cottage, some money in the bank, not a lot in itself.'

'More than we've got,' Gwen Woodcock said. 'And you want to throw us out on the street, even after all we've done for you.'

'Done for me?' Margaret said. 'You've paid your rent, nothing more. And then you're talking to the police, telling them about my private business.'

'Only because you threatened us. How are you with a chainsaw, Margaret? You're strong enough to have cut up Sheila.'

'Be quiet, all of you,' Desdemona Foster said. For once the woman who said very little spoke up, her squeaky voice replaced by a resilient and robust tone. Everyone in the pub took notice. Her husband, Hamish, the recipient of her invective on more than one occasion behind closed doors, only looked at her. He removed his hand from her shoulder.

'The floor's yours, Desdemona,' Baxter said.

'Four people have died, and of those, only one has someone charged with the crime. Don't you realise it? One of us is a murderer, maybe two. The police suspect Barry and Gwen, but there's no proof. Rupert hated Gloria and Sheila, not so much Bert, and they're all dead. Maybe Rupert killed them. No doubt he had a good reason.'

'I would have killed Gloria on the day of James's death, that's true, for what she said. James was a sensitive soul. He only saw the good in people, not that there's much in here. And Desdemona, why now? You always sit there impassively listening to the verbiage on that side of the bar, and now you decide to speak.'

'You can't talk to my wife like that,' Hamish Foster said.

'I can and I will,' Rupert said. 'Desdemona's got something to say. She may not say much normally, but we need to hear it now, unpleasant home truths if that's to be the case.'

'The police come out here every day, Inspector Tremayne and Sergeant Yarwood. They ask a few questions, find some answers, but they don't get the full truth, do they?'

'We answer them as we can,' Eustace Upminster said. His wife sat still, not looking up, not looking around.

'That's what I mean. Someone in this room is a murderer. If that person has killed three and can sit here calmly, then they are a cruel and calculating person.'

'What do you mean?' Gwen said.

'If they can kill three, they can kill four or five. Their original motive may no longer be valid. If it was Barry or Rupert who killed the first three, then they had a reason to hate, but what if now someone's got a taste for it?'

'A bloodlust?'

'Why not? Don't those who slaughter animals on the farm become ambivalent to the process? Don't men in war become blasé about taking another life, committing atrocities? It could be that our killer is the same. He could be here now saying little or saying a lot, and all the time eyeing his next victim up and down, imagining the knife going in, the bullet penetrating the body, the chainsaw severing it limb by limb.'

'For Christ's sake, stop it,' Gladys Upminster said. 'Enough is enough. Haven't we suffered enough? Desdemona, you need to stop watching those inane television detective series. They're making you crazy, imagining things when they aren't there. Isn't it obvious who's guilty?'

'Who?' Rupert said. 'Are you about to say that it was either Barry or me?'

'Who else had the motive? And Margaret's next, that's who. What will it be for her? How will she die?'

'You've a sense of the dramatic,' Baxter said. Gladys's husband said nothing, only glared at his wife. 'Your son died in an accident and you blame yourself. It's unhinged you. I hated Gloria and would have done her harm at the time, but I've moved on. I suggest you do as well.'

'He's right, Gladys,' Eustace Upminster said. He raised his glass to Baxter for another pint of beer.

'I've killed no one,' Barry Woodcock said. 'You're the one with the secrets,' he said, directing his eyes at Gladys.

'What do you mean?' Gladys replied.

'I knew your son. We were friendly, and sure, he was wild, but it was you with your constant nagging at him to shape up, get a haircut, find a good woman, a decent job. You drove him to despair, yet he said nothing; just stormed out of your house and let off steam. It was an accident, but you were the trigger. Accept the truth and move on. I lost James, a decent man and a friend.'

Gladys Upminster said nothing. Eustace looked at Barry and mouthed a thank you. Someone had finally told his wife the truth, someone other than him. He hoped that the grieving process would commence and that his wife would move on, rather than listening to the endless droning on, first of Gloria and then Sheila and now Margaret.

'Are we going to tell the police the truth about this village? The lies, the hidden secrets? Or are we all going to sit here and let one of us murder us all?' Gwen said.

'Very well,' Margaret said. 'The truth.'

'Let's start with you, Margaret. You're the de facto leader of this village, not through any true authority, but through your wealth.'

'My life is private, not that you'd respect it.'

'Just because I told the police about you and Rupert. Look at you two, opposite sides of the bar, pretending to have nothing in common, but we all know.'

'Not everyone.'

'We're not stupid, Margaret,' Hamish said. 'We all know about you two, and besides, what does it matter? Just stupid old-fashioned pride that no one's spoken of it, and you and Rupert act as if touching the other would be akin to catching a disease.'

'It's our private business,' Rupert said.

'Agreed,' Eustace Upminster said, 'but if it has a bearing on who the murderer is, then it's not.'

'I don't see how it's relevant,' Margaret said.

'That's the point, you don't,' Gwen Woodcock said. 'But you're not a trained police officer. Maybe it is relevant, maybe the other secrets that this village holds so close are.'

'My relationship with James was not platonic,' Barry Woodcock blurted out.

'I was correct,' Margaret said. 'I know what I saw.'

'I was young, impressionable, and I was very fond of James.'

'Gwen, any comment?' Rupert Baxter asked.

'We have no secrets, Barry and me. I've always known the truth.'

'Yet you constantly denied it, even to the police.'

'It's a secret, and as with Margaret, a secret we would have preferred not to tell anyone about.'

'Has anyone anything more to say?' Eustace Upminster asked. 'Does anyone want to admit to murder? Maybe we should call Tremayne and Sergeant Yarwood to join us? We need to stop the murders and in here seems the best opportunity. Hamish, you've not said much. You could have carved up Sheila. She was Rupert's blood relative on their father's side. Now there was a man who used to put it about. No sneaking up to Margaret's pile of rubble. It's a wonder you two entwined don't bring the rest of it down.'

'Scurrilous and unworthy,' Baxter said. 'Margaret is a fine woman, not someone for your titillation.'

'Strange bedfellows, that's all I'm saying. And what about Gloria, were you sleeping with her? Was she jealous? Did she have to die, so you and Margaret could continue cavorting? The truths are coming out now, no need to hold back.'

'Upminster, you're a bore and a pig. Your attempt at humour is in the worst of taste. I was not involved with Gloria or anyone else in this village, only Margaret, and only in the last year.'

'But as teenagers, you were.'

'We all were. You were with Gloria and Stephanie yourself, and don't deny it.'

'I'm not, but it was innocent love, no more than fumbling in the dark.'

'What I have with Margaret is pure, so don't attempt to imply it's anything else.'

'And with Sheila?'

'If you must know, I was in love with her. I would have married her back when I was younger, but then the issue of a shared father doomed the relationship. We remained friendly, if distant, from then on. We disagreed on many things, the same as I do with Margaret, but we can't help who we love and who we do not. Eustace, the truth about you and Gladys?'

'We're going,' Gladys said, as she grabbed her husband and dragged him out of the pub. After that, the pub slowly emptied. The Fosters left after Hamish had drunk another two pints of beer; Desdemona had reverted to type, and she barely said another word. The Woodcocks left arm-in-arm.

In the pub, Rupert and Margaret remained. 'A strange night,' Rupert said.

'No more than usual. You know that you are a wicked man,' Margaret said. She smiled at her paramour. 'We make no sense.'

'None at all. Will you stay the night?'

'Seeing that it's no longer a secret, then yes.'

'It never was. We should make it legal.'

'In time. Once the deaths stop.'

'Will they?'

'Who knows?' Margaret said.

Chapter 18

Louise Regan, the head of Forensics, peered at Tremayne through her thick-framed glasses. 'You what?' she said.

'It's only a thought, but what are the chances of finding anything?' Tremayne said. Clare was with him, the question of Tichborne's guilt for two deaths still fresh in their minds.

'You've read the report, Tichborne's wife died of natural causes, nothing untoward in itself, although she was relatively young. She was still subjected to an examination by a doctor. Not as exhaustive as if foul play had been suspected, but the woman had a history of ailments, a weak heart. The police were not involved as no suspicion surrounded her death. Haven't you got enough to deal with at the present time without exhuming her?'

'We do, but if Tichborne is correct in what he said, then it's possible murder, or at least involuntary manslaughter.'

'The paperwork will be extensive, and there'll be delays. The woman died eleven years ago, so I'd not hold out for much proof of anything. We know the drugs she was on, and there may be traces, but ascertaining whether they were at an overdose level will be almost impossible to prove conclusively. Unless it's critical, I'd suggest you leave the woman where she is.'

Tremayne had followed through on a possible avenue of enquiry, although he, like Clare, was not too keen on the idea. And Louise Regan was right, the paperwork would be horrendous, the results probably inconclusive.

The rectory had revealed that the Reverend Tichborne was a fastidious man, the items of cutlery in the kitchen drawer all in their correct places: the forks to the left, and then the knives, followed by the spoons. In the cupboards, the condiments were lined up in their jars and bottles, the labels pointing forward, the cups and saucers neatly stacked. Clare, who had had a cursory look over the place, marvelled at how anyone could be so neat. She tried in her cottage, but the hours she worked precluded such attention to detail. She had considered hiring someone to come in on a casual basis to clean, but so far had refrained on account of the cost. She had adopted a regimen of doubling the repayments on the mortgage to shorten the payout period from the original twenty-five years down to less than half, and it was paying off. A cleaner would have impeded her plan. Nothing more had been found in the rectory, except for a large collection of photos of the vicar and his wife; some on holiday, some in the church, more when he had been ordained, and then her as the blushing bride. Apart from that, no sign of any other woman in the building, which was not surprising. In fact, only a few people in the

149

village could ever remember entering the rectory, and most meetings of the churchgoers, and those interested in Sunday school for the children and organising an annual fair, occurred in the vestry. Tichborne still languished behind bars, and Stephanie Underwood's house had revealed that Tichborne was more than likely the murderer, a strand of wool from a jumper having been found near to where the dead woman had been. The forensic analysis had confirmed that it matched clothing that had been found in the rectory. Also, a smudged fingerprint found on a door handle at the woman's cottage was almost certainly Tichborne's, although when it had been placed there was open to conjecture. The case was tightening on Tichborne, although Tremayne still had his doubts, but would not voice them at this time.

The get-together in the village pub had been described to Tremayne and Clare by Baxter, who, feeling some contrition about revealing the details of the interview between Tichborne and the two police officers, was going out of his way to make amends.

Tremayne realised that another visit to the village of Compton was necessary, but to do what? To ask what? Everyone had been questioned, nothing new had come from the pub get-together, apart from confirmation that Barry Woodcock and James Baxter were intimately involved, the reason for Gloria Wiggins' denouncement proven.

Tremayne sat in his office, the ubiquitous laptop beckoning him, its charms failing. He called in Clare. It was always the same, Tremayne knew, when sitting in the office. The itchy feet, the need to get out there and stir the pot, ruffle a few feathers, but policing was becoming bureaucratised, and more could be achieved from the relative comfort of an office than out in the field.

Tremayne missed the good old days when instinct and experience counted for plenty; now everyone was an instant expert, even his sergeant who could tell him almost as much as Forensics and Pathology by searching on Google.

'Yarwood, what now?' Tremayne said. Clare could see him champing at the bit.

'No leads to follow up on, just conjecture,' Clare said.

'But now we know that Woodcock and James Baxter were more than hand-shaking friends, and everyone knows about Margaret Wilmot and Rupert Baxter. Those two revelations must have opened some wounds, and Gwen Woodcock, she supported her husband, but had she known the truth, or was it just an immediate reaction? Important to know, don't you think?'

'Important, but what does it tell us? The pigs where Bert Blatchford died would make better witnesses. It's a shame we can't ask them.'

'They may well be better than some of the others in the village,' Tremayne said.

'Some? I'd say all of them, even Tichborne who's still holding back.'

'Forget Tichborne. We've exhausted him for now. Who else is there that's not figured in our investigation?'

'No one of interest. It's a small village, and everyone's been interviewed, and more than once. Could it be someone else, someone unknown in the village, the missing piece?'

'It's not likely. Personally, I'm not too keen on Baxter, too smart by half, and he knows what's going on. And this relationship with Margaret, bizarre.'

'Is it? Two lonely people in a lonely village thrown together by fate and by history.'

Tremayne got up from his seat; he needed out. As he made for the exit, Moulton waylaid him with the inevitable questioning about the investigation, a gentle enquiry about his health.

'The man's getting ready to try for my retirement again,' Tremayne said to Clare after Moulton had left.

'You'll resist,' Clare said.

'I'm not so sure. I'm getting tired of working here, and the atmosphere in the building's not what it used to be. I could take up golf, even become a stamp collector, something like that.'

'You'd be dead within the year.'

'It's just an idea, but each time Moulton comes around there's another sweetener. Jean's interested in travel.'

'The man who regards any more than ten miles from Salisbury as a trek into the unknown. Hardly your style, is it?'

'It could be with Jean. Travel broadens the mind, that's what they say.'

'Your interest extends no further than policing and betting on three-legged horses. What mind-broadening experience will travel bring to you?'

'You're right, but the investigations don't get easier, just more obscure. The murderers are either smarter, or I'm getting dumber.'

'It's not you, it's them. Anyone with a computer can research forensics, how to carry out the perfect murder, how to avoid leaving evidence.'

'Our murderer is smart?'

'He could be.'

'Or she? There's no reason to exclude a woman,' Tremayne said. He and Clare were outside the office. For once, the sky was clear and blue, even though there was a cold breeze.

'We could access their internet habits,' Clare said.

'And see who's been looking at sites they shouldn't?'

'Not that, but sites that delve into the intricacies of policing, forensics, and how to conceal evidence.'

'Stephanie Underwood was an avid surfer of the internet. Check her history. She could have killed Gloria Wiggins, and her statement that she didn't hear anything still has an air of unlikelihood about it.'

Tremayne continued out to Compton. He needed to talk to Rupert Baxter. Clare returned to the office to focus on internet records. She needed a judge to authorise examination of the woman's surfing activities and then found that the internet coverage in the village was not the best. A newly-installed tower up on the main road had assisted, but it had not been in place when the first murder was committed. Stephanie Underwood's surfing habits were easily obtained. She had an eclectic taste in subjects to research: medieval history, particularly pertaining to Salisbury and especially to Compton, and an interest in weaponry and crime and the perfect murder.

Clare also received permission to access the internet history of several other people in the village. The Blatchfords were not on the list, nor were the Woodcocks, as neither husband nor wife had a computer or a smartphone set up for data. The Upminsters, especially Eustace, did, as did Margaret Wilmot and Rupert Baxter. The Reverend Tichborne did have a laptop, and it had not taken long to find that his searching on the internet was primarily for preparation of the droning sermons that he gave, apart from a couple of email addresses that he occasionally sent messages to.

'I always knew the truth,' Baxter said, when Tremayne asked the question. The two men were holding a pint of beer each. Tremayne was propped up on a stool on his side of the bar; Baxter was leaning forward, one of his elbows resting on the bar.

'That's not what you told us.'

'It wasn't that important, and James was my brother. I didn't want to add to the local gossip, and besides, it was Margaret who had told the truth.'

'What is it with her? Tremayne said. 'No disrespect, but you and she don't fit the mould of young lovers. Margaret's a terse woman, not a lot of humour, and you're gregarious, even if you've got a mouth that never closes.'

'That's the fit. Sometimes, I like it quiet and less extrovert; Margaret has spent her life, even her childhood, with her mind being stoked with this feudal idea of the Lord and Master. Her father was a tyrant, used to hit Margaret until he had hammered into her what you see. I can't blame her for what she is, and she is a good woman. Somehow, the two of us come together in that one place, and then it's fine. No pretensions, no discussions about what ails the world or this village, no discussion of who killed who.'

'It makes for a difficult relationship.'

'It does, but it's fun. I'm not one for a mealy-mouthed subservient woman. I had one of those, and she did a runner, took my child as well. With Margaret, I'm on safe ground.'

Tremayne thought the man's explanation plausible. And besides, there were other more important facts to be ascertained.

'Tichborne? What do you reckon to him murdering Stephanie Underwood?' Tremayne asked.

'What's to say? It came as a bit of a shock when he confessed to her murder, and now, the word is that the death of his wife was suspicious.'

'You've not heard that from me.'

'It's the word in the village. I can remember her, a pale woman, taller than him, a few years older.'

'Did she talk much?'

'Only down at the church and occasionally on the street. I never had more than a cursory chat with her, the weather, how was she, that sort of thing. She never came in the pub, strict teetotaller, and Tichborne always looked worn down by her. He was much more open after she had gone.'

'Open? Tichborne? He's not one of life's most sociable, even now.'

'Compared to when his wife was alive, he's a changed man. Before, he'd not say boo to a goose and certainly said very little to anyone. Locked himself up in the rectory and the church most of the time, apart from when he was out visiting a sick or elderly parishioner. A decent man, even if he wasn't best-suited for his vocation. But then, I wasn't meant to be a publican. I had dreams of academia, but the family tradition placed this in my hands, as James wasn't willing to take it on.'

'It could have been sold,' Tremayne said. 'And what area of academia?'

'Tradition meant a lot to my parents, even if fidelity didn't to my father.'

'How did James feel about Sheila Blatchford being a relative, a half-sister?'

'It wasn't spoken about, and I'm not sure he knew. My father told me before he died, knowing that I was more open-minded, but James was younger, more idealistic. I don't think my father would have wanted a disapproving son, especially James.'

'Why James and not you?'

'James was his favourite. Everyone's favourite, in fact. An attractive child, a handsome youth. And he had a pleasant manner that drew people to him. My parents idolised him, although they were good to me. You can't help having favourites, can you?'

'I suppose not.' It reminded Tremayne of his own childhood, the elder sister, wealthy and living up in London. It had been years since he had seen her, and she was growing old and not in good health. A visit to see her suddenly seemed important.

'You'd not know it by looking at me, that I've a genius-level intellect,' Baxter said.

'You hide it well. This village hides its secrets, the same as you.'

'It does. I still read a lot and study, but I wasn't the most motivated. It's a damn nuisance having intelligence.'

'I've never had that problem.'

'Inspector Tremayne, you're smarter than you think. You observe, listen, apply logic. To me that's intelligence. What I've got is a head full of ideas, some coherent, others fanciful.'

'What if you applied your fanciful ideas to this village? What do you come up with? And did Tichborne kill his wife?'

'He could have. The man should have gone through the grieving process, but when she died, he didn't act in that way. For the first couple of weeks, he was in the pub every night. Just a glass of wine, nothing stronger, but before, she would have kept him out. I suspected that he may be a man partial to the drink, but I've never seen him drunk.'

'There were a few bottles of whisky and vodka down at the rectory,' Tremayne said. 'No sign that he was heavily into them.'

'I don't get why Tichborne killed Stephanie,' Baxter said. He had poured himself another pint of beer, given one to Tremayne.

'According to him, Stephanie knew that he had killed his wife, and she could prove it.'

'How and why? Stephanie wasn't that sort of person. A gossip, but harmless, and no one disliked her, not even Gloria, and they lived next door to each other. A strange pair, the two of them. One frivolous, the other severe and demanding.'

'Any different to you and Margaret?'

'Not really, and Margaret takes this fire and brimstone stuff seriously. A clever woman, yet she gets involved in such nonsense, even acted friendly with Gloria and Sheila, not that she had anything in common with them.'

'Did Margaret like the two of them?'

'Margaret's a complex woman. She'd like to be more approachable and agreeable, but it's in her heritage, the stiff upper lip, the talking down to the peasants.'

'Are you a peasant, Baxter?'

'Not me, although my heritage is in trade, a despised profession to the landed gentry. This pub has had a Baxter behind the bar for over two centuries. Margaret likes Gwen Woodcock, although you'd not realise it. It's Barry that Margaret has a problem with.'

'On account of him and James?'

'Margaret was married once, a long time ago. He lived in a village not far from here, and it didn't last for long. It turned out that his inclinations were not for her, but for others.'

'James?'

'It was a long time ago, and James would have only been young, and it wasn't Barry either. Margaret found out on the wedding night.'

'Not consummated?'

'Margaret won't tell you, but you needed to know the truth. I'm telling you for her. It made her an embittered woman, and for years she's lived in that old house, mainly on her own, apart from Gwen going up there occasionally to clean around a bit, and to help out if she could.'

'But there's no overt signs of affection between them.'

'There can't be, not from Margaret. And you've met Gwen enough times. A humble woman, looks after Barry and the children, although no money to talk of.'

'Does Gwen know that Margaret likes her?'

'She does. Why do you think Gwen told you about Margaret and me?'

'You're telling the story,' Tremayne said. He was halfway into his third pint. He was driving, and it wouldn't do for a police officer to be caught over the limit. He determined to drink no more.

'Margaret would let her reticence condemn her before she'd reveal the truth about her and her family. To her, certain things must not be spoken of to outsiders and those below her station. Don't get the impression that she's a snob, but her former husband, her and me, are not for general discourse.'

'If we charged her with murder, she'd still hold back on any evidence to prove her innocence if it besmirched the Wilmot name?'

'That's about it. I've spoken to her about it, tried to get through to her that it's the twenty-first century, and people don't care about a person's peccadilloes, their family. I've told you about mine, warts and all.'

'You kept quiet about your brother.'

'Not really. I preferred not to talk about it, but I would have if it had been necessary. That's a big difference to Margaret.'

'You'll defend her, as will Gwen?'

'We will.'

'But Gwen's being evicted?'

'Margaret's trying to force Barry to shape up, but he's really hopeless. He'll just let life pass on by, and if he's out of the farm, then he'll throw himself on the mercy of the village. Someone will give him somewhere for them to live.'

'A strange way to live.'

'That's Barry. In the end, Margaret will probably relent, and Gwen knows this, but Barry's too slow on the uptake to understand and to do something about it.'

'It makes him an unlikely murderer,' Tremayne said.

'It does. Barry couldn't kill anyone, although Gwen's more resilient.'

'It could be her, is that what you're saying?'

'Not Gwen. She'd not do anything to come between her and her children. A good woman who married the wrong man.'

'Who was the right man?'

'Not me. And besides, Gwen wouldn't have fitted into academia. She's a village woman, and I wanted the bright lights of Oxford.'

'There are not many bright lights in Oxford.'

'You know what I mean. I've a degree from there, a couple, in fact.'

'Then why back here, family tradition or not?'

'The pub was here, and once I was back, I found that I preferred it to the stuffy, cloistered atmosphere of university life. I carry on my research when I get a chance, publish the occasional paper, quantum physics. Here I can do that, and I'm free to work at my own pace, go fishing when I want.'

'And to seduce Margaret,' Tremayne added.

'That as well. We talk about my research sometimes. I don't think she understands much of what I write about, but she takes an interest.'

After leaving Baxter, Tremayne found Clare at the police station with her laptop and a monitor. She looked up as he entered. 'You'd better see this,' she said.

'Margaret Wilmot likes to surf the internet, nothing much of interest, apart from renovations of heritage-listed properties and finance. Hamish Foster's into farming and his wife is interested in fashion. Gladys Upminster appears to have a morbid interest with death and the occult and the loss of a loved one.'

'Makes sense that she'd be into that,' Tremayne said. He had taken a seat to one side of Clare and had put on a pair of glasses to focus on the monitor. It was still blurred: another visit to the opticians was on the cards.

'Eustace Upminster is the main one of interest,' Clare said. Tremayne could see that she had a smug look on her face. 'He's been using false names to log on, but his IP's a giveaway. He's been checking out sites related to his wife's issues.'

'That's to be expected. What else?'

'YouTube videos on police investigative techniques, how to commit the perfect murder, how to avoid leaving evidence.'

'No doubt a few in the village have been doing that as well. Have you checked on Rupert Baxter?'

'After what you told me on the phone driving back to the office, I did.'

'And?'

'We knew about the degrees, and yes, the man is involved with academia. I tried to read one of his published papers, gave up not long after I read his name. Mathematics was never my strongest subject, but he's way ahead of anything I understand. Possible murderer?'

'They all are. Anything else from Baxter?'

'He's checked out what we're doing, following up on unsolved murders, how to avoid a jail sentence, that sort of thing.'

'Upminster, capable with computer technology?'

'About average. If he was good, he would have blocked his use of the internet, made it difficult for us to trace him.'

'Can you do that?'

'Is that me, or a general question?'

'Both.'

'I probably could to some extent. An expert could work his way through, discover it was me, and the internet into Compton is not extensive. Elimination of potential users could trace it back to him.'

'It could be his wife.'

'It could, but I'm discounting her for now. The questions and the subjects are more male-oriented.'

'How do you read Eustace Upminster, a gut feeling?' Tremayne said. 'His wife can't be a bundle of fun.'

'Not like Margaret Wilmot from what we've been hearing.'

Tremayne sat back on his chair and took out a packet of cigarettes. He realised that it was an automatic reaction, and neither the police station regulations nor Clare approved of his habit. 'Outside,' he said.

'What's your feeling about Eustace Upminster?' Tremayne repeated the question that had not been answered due to his need to light up. He had tried to moderate his smoking and had had some success, but the need remained, especially in a time of stress, and that was what they had in bucket-loads. Not only was Baxter in line for further questioning, so were Eustace and Gladys Upminster.

'A decent man with a troubled wife. Not sure how anyone deals with the death of a child, even if he was wild. It's taken me years to get over Harry's death, but time moves on. You never forget though, the quiet moments. I'd rather be at work than at home, even after so long. Even now, I have trouble going past where he lived, the pub he owned, the places we visited together.'

'But you've managed.'

'Gladys Upminster's a worrier, a woman who constantly remembers the past, afraid to let go. That's why she's with the fire and brimstoners. They take her out of herself, remind her that it was not her fault.'

Tremayne smoked half his cigarette, stubbed out the remainder on the bin, and took a mint from his pocket.

'They'll not do you much good after you've smoked that old weed,' Clare said.

'Don't go on, Yarwood. One of life's small pleasures. You can't begrudge me that.'

'It's no pleasure for me, and what does Jean say when you get home of a night?'

'No smoking back there. She's worse than you.'

Chapter 19

The Upminsters' farm was calm, although not for long, as a gaggle of geese came from around the back of the barn at the sound of Tremayne and Clare's arrival.

'They'd wake the dead,' Tremayne said.

'No shortage of those in Compton,' Clare said glibly.

The farmhouse was neat and tidy, an old dog sleeping close to the front door. It took no notice of the visitors. Tremayne knocked on the door, the first time a gentle tap, the second time more heavily. Eventually, the door opened, and Gladys Upminster stood there. She was dressed as if she was about to go into town.

'He's not here,' Gladys said.

'We want to see you both,' Clare said.

'We had an argument.'

'A common occurrence?'

The woman did not answer the question. 'There were a few home truths at Baxter's pub. I never knew about Baxter and Margaret, I swear that I didn't,' she said instead.

'How did it affect you?'

'I placed great faith in Gloria and Sheila. I saw some worth in Margaret, but she's disappointed me. All that proselytising, and what is she, a fornicator, and not even a ring on her finger, and with that horrible man. It doesn't bear thinking about.'

'They're over the age of consent,' Clare said.

'I place great faith in one man, one woman, and the marital bed. How can I respect a woman who behaves in such a way?'

'You accept people for what they are, good and bad,' Tremayne said. 'Can we come in?'

Inside the house was not much warmer than when they had been standing on the doorstep. The two police officers made no comment. Clare thought the temperature was the same as the woman's heart.

'And where is your husband?' Clare said. She had her hands in her jacket pocket to overcome the cold rising from the stone floor.

'He's around somewhere.'

'Do you use the internet?'

'I've got an iPad. Eustace spends more time than I do, but he's got a computer upstairs.'

'Is the farm profitable?'

'It is, but that's not why you're here, is it?'

'We've been checking on the internet usage in Compton,' Clare said. 'We know about what you view, mostly related to the death of a loved one, that sort of thing.'

'And Eustace?'

'Some farming, but there are other sites he's visited which are related to police investigations, murder. Do you know about this?'

'Most in the village would be guilty of checking up on what you've been trying to do, not very successfully judging by the results.'

'These investigations can take time,' Tremayne said by way of defence.

'We speak amongst ourselves, curious as to who it may be. We're all scared, although not many of us are showing it. Eustace is one of those who's worried.'

'How about you?'

'Death would be a blessing. I only hope it's quick and painless when it comes.'

'An unnatural reaction,' Clare said. 'Time has moved on since your son died. It is for you to come to terms with it, and to look back on him with fondness, to remember the good times, to forget the bad.'

'I can't. I hated him, I always did. A malevolent weasel of a child, a vicious, argumentative and lazy man later on. That car he was driving, we gave it to him, hoping that he'd get out and find a job, a good woman, but what does he do? He kills himself in it. If we hadn't given him the damn thing, he'd still be alive and blighting our lives.'

'Does your husband feel the same way?'

'He's done what you suggested, moved on. He now talks about him in loving tones, not something he could do when he was alive. There was evil in that child, I'm telling you.'

'Biblical?'

'I don't know. I just know that I found some solace with Gloria and the others, even Margaret, and look at what she has become.'

166

'A jaundiced view of the world, Mrs Upminster,' Tremayne said.

'An honest view. I am not long for this world, I know that. And Eustace, he won't care much.'

'On the contrary,' Clare said. 'We believe that he cares for your well-being more than you give him credit for. It doesn't seem that you respond to his concerns.'

'Where can we find your husband?' Tremayne said.

'He's outside somewhere. He left over an hour ago.'

'What was the argument about?'

'Eustace was telling me it was time to move on, the same as you. I'm afraid that I called him a few names that I shouldn't, accused him of murdering Gloria and Sheila.'

'How is Eustace with a chainsaw?'

'He's capable. He doesn't say much normally, but he's tough. He'd been in the military and seen active service. He killed then, he could kill now.'

'We're aware of his military record,' Clare said. 'Some medals, but he was not on the front line.'

'He won't talk about it, but I've seen his record upstairs. There are things in there that you wouldn't want to see. Oh, yes, Eustace is a killer, and I wouldn't put it past him being a murderer, not that I'd tell you normally, but he said things that no man should say to his wife.'

'It may not be my position to comment,' Clare said, 'but you are not a nice person. Married couples have arguments, the same as other people, but they control that anger, put it in context. You, Mrs Upminster, have an unnatural reluctance to face reality, whereas your husband may have grieved as much as you in the past.'

'I don't need to listen to you telling me what to do and say.'

Fired up and furious, Gladys Upminster grabbed a knife from the kitchen sink and lunged at Clare. She moved to one side, the blade harmlessly moving into fresh air, and with Tremayne grabbing the woman's wrist and wrenching the knife from her clenched hand.

'Well done,' Tremayne said to Clare.

He looked over at Gladys Upminster who was now sitting on a chair. 'It appears that you are capable of violence. You may not have killed the women, but Bert Blatchford was murdered with a knife, very similar to the one you just used.'

'She had no right to speak like that to me.'

'She had every right to know what you were capable of. Everyone in this village hides their true feelings well. No one tells us the truth, yet they expect us to find the murderer. This is a small village. You must have your suspicions.'

Clare put on the kettle and found some tea bags in a cupboard and milk in the fridge. She gave a mug of tea to Gladys Upminster. The woman responded weakly with a smile and a thank you.

'Eustace killed Gloria, I'm sure of it. That's what the argument was about,' the man's wife resignedly said. Clare was not proud about how she had riled the woman, but she and Tremayne had agreed that pussy-footing around was not going to provide results and that the village community had locked them out of their innermost secrets. With one person opening up, the others would do as well. It had been a hard-fought battle, and now they had a woman at the end of her wits, a woman who was capable of anything, even murder.

'Why?'

'Because of her hold over me. Because he was sleeping with her, and she wasn't going to let him go.'

'We've no record of any relationship between your husband and Gloria. All indications were that they did not like each other.'

'It's Compton. Who hates and who loves don't apply. Secretive they were, thought that I didn't know, not that I can blame Gloria. He was a good catch, and there was no way he was coming near me after our son had died.'

'How long have you known?'

'Long enough. Eight to nine months, probably. I could smell her on him, and the way they didn't look at each other in the pub and on a Sunday at the church. It was the same with Margaret and Rupert. My husband's right, I'm not a good person to be around, but after he had killed Gloria, then the village changed. Before that we were a fractious community, but somehow we survived, but her death alienated people, brought into play tensions that had been subdued. Margaret may have been the money in this village, but Gloria was the glue. No doubt you don't understand, but that's the way we've always been. Apart from the Reverend Tichborne, hardly any other families had come into the village. We're the same families that have lived here for generations.'

'Why are you now telling us that your husband is guilty of murder?'

'So that you'll understand why I killed him.'

'When, and where is he?'

'Outside, behind the barn where the geese came from.'

Tremayne left the house, making a phone call for a patrol car to come to Compton, and for someone to stay with Gladys Upminster. Whether she was guilty of murder or not, she could not be left on her own. A full appraisal of her medical and mental health was needed. Another phone call to Jim Hughes to forewarn him that the crime scene team may be required. Before ending the call, Tremayne took one look in front of him. 'Confirmed,' he said.

Tremayne moved to where the body of the dead man was, a knife in his back, the same as it had been with Bert Blatchford. Tremayne gently prodded the body with his hand. The man moved, a muffled groan.

'Are you okay?' Tremayne said. A stupid question he realised. A person with a knife in the back was not going to be okay, but he still had a chance. Tremayne phoned for Emergency Services to send an ambulance, briefly describing the condition of the man on the ground. Clare took instructions from Tremayne and cuffed the man's wife before putting her in the back of her car. She had not been charged as yet, but Tremayne needed Clare free to assist, not burdened with a psychotic and disturbed woman who had knifed one person, had been willing to knife another and would perhaps try for a second time.

Twelve minutes later, a patrol car. They took responsibility for Gladys Upminster as well as establishing the crime scene, not that there was any doubt as to who the guilty party was. A medic, the same woman who had attended to Clare when she had been attacked at Stephanie Underwood's house, stabilised Eustace Upminster and transferred him to Salisbury Hospital.

Rupert Baxter appeared within minutes, closely followed by the Woodcocks. Margaret Wilmot, from her house over the hill, arrived after a call from Baxter.

Gladys Upminster was not guilty of premeditated murder, although she was capable of anger and hatred, and a prejudice against anyone who did not fit her idealised notion of decency. But Gloria Wiggins' death had required a stronger person than her, as would Sheila's, and if the woman's ineffective use of a knife on Clare and her husband was indicative, she did not kill Bert Blatchford either.

Tremayne and Clare remained out at Compton until late. Gladys's statement about her husband had to be checked. As expected the village clammed up on whether Eustace and Gloria had been involved. Clare's opinion was that they were not, and the clearly mentally unstable woman had clutched at straws, taken one and one and made three.

No one could ever remember Gloria expressing interest in any man, at least since her teens, when Rupert had admitted to being a bit of a lad in the village, and to have spent time with both Gloria and her next-door neighbour. Harmless adolescent hormones, had been his comment.

'We still need to interview Gladys Upminster at Bemerton Road,' Clare said.

'She'll wait for tomorrow.' It was one in the morning, not unusual for the two officers. Tremayne was exhausted, dozing on the way home to Wilton, and Clare was not much better, but she was driving. Even though it was late, supper was on the table. Jean invited Clare in as well, and she fell asleep in a chair at the house. Jean put a blanket over her and left her there.

'Two cooked breakfasts tomorrow,' she said to Tremayne as they both climbed the stairs to their bedroom.

Chapter 20

Eustace Upminster briefly acknowledged Tremayne and Clare with a nod of his head as they entered his room at Salisbury Hospital. He was not sitting up in bed, which was expected after a knife wound in the back. Instead he was propped to one side, the area of injury cocooned by pillows. It was clear that he was sedated. The knife, as the doctor explained, had been deflected by the braces that Upminster wore under his jacket to hold up the loose-fitting trousers that he preferred to wear around the farm. If he had been coherent, he would have said that he relished the freedom they gave him, especially on a hot day when a belt around the waist would have chafed.

'Gladys?' the man weakly muttered.

'She's been charged with attempted murder,' Clare said.

'It was my fault. You can't hold her, it'll be the death of her.'

'Unfortunately, the law's the law,' Tremayne said. 'She's committed a criminal act, but mitigating circumstances will be taken into consideration.'

A nurse standing to one side attempted to intervene, although Tremayne brushed her away. Some questions needed to be asked, and whether the man was in a condition to be interviewed or not, those questions had to be answered.

'Your wife made a damning accusation about you,' Tremayne said. 'Accused you of carrying on an affair with Gloria Wiggins.'

'That's Gladys, I'm afraid. Too much time on her hands, too much time to dwell on her life and our son,' Upminster said.

'This is too much,' the nurse said. 'Mr Upminster is in intensive care, his condition requires rest, not the two of you.'

'Unfortunately, we've got four murders, one attempted, and Mr Upminster's right in the middle of it and his wife's in jail. No doubt he'd want to see her comfortable and hopefully released on bail.'

'Is that possible?' Upminster said.

'It depends on you, doesn't it?'

'There was nothing between Gloria and me. Maybe when we were younger, just teens, but the woman changed as she got older. A tyrant at the end. I tolerated her on account of Gladys, but I couldn't abide her, and now look what's happened.'

'Would you consider you and your wife to be close?' Clare said.

'As close as any married couple after so many years together. We used to argue when our son was alive, more often than not over him, but nowadays the arguments are rare. Most of the time it's long periods of silent, sullen glances at each other, but she had got this idea about Gloria and me.'

'She accused you of murdering the woman.'

'Don't listen to her. She has these ideas, and then she spends hours on her own in the house just looking into space, sobbing and then laughing out loud. They wanted me to put her in care at one stage while they counselled her through her grief. The idea appealed, and I thought she'd go at one stage, but then she decided against it. Not that anyone could force her and she wasn't a threat to society.'

'She is now.'

'Then maybe some good will come of it. If time in an institution is what is necessary then we'll be all the better for it.'

'Did your wife kill anyone?' Tremayne asked. He could see the man wilting, his eyes close to shutting.

'No.'

'And what about you? If it's true about your affair with Gloria, and we'll be checking, then you could have killed her. And we've now got your wife, a proven knife attacker. Bert Blatchford was killed with a knife. Why?'

'What do you mean?'

'In your incestuous community, what else is there that we don't know? Did Bert Blatchford have some hold over you and your wife? We always assumed that Barry Woodcock and Rupert Baxter were the most likely guilty parties, but now we have a vicar for one of the murders. Gladys could have killed Bert, you could have killed the others.'

'I could have, so could my wife, but we didn't.'

After the husband, there was the wife to interview. Gladys Upminster was brought into the interview room at Bemerton Road Police Station, a lawyer of her acquaintance attending for her, and the inevitable questions, the inconclusive answers.

'At your house, before we found your husband collapsed on the ground, you were willing to condemn him as a murderer and an adulterer, but now your story has changed,' Tremayne said.

'It was an unfortunate chain of events. He made me angry, I lashed out. It's as simple as that.'

'With a knife? Do you do that often? Resolve your disputes with a display of weaponry? And why did you lunge at Sergeant Yarwood?'

'She was annoying me,' Gladys Upminster said. Her lawyer sat to one side, a faraway look on his face. Clare thought that under the circumstances the woman could have chosen someone more dynamic.

'Your husband will live, no thanks to you,' Tremayne said.

'I didn't want to harm him, not really, but he said some terrible things.'

'Such as?'

'I don't want to repeat them.'

'Mrs Upminster, you've been charged with attempted murder. Whether that charge is reduced to attempted manslaughter or even results in a non-custodial sentence is up to you.'

'Very well. I did accuse him of having an affair with Gloria. A woman knows, you must realise that.'

'But why Gloria?'

'They were close when they were younger, and he married me on the rebound. We were both twenty back then, and our son was on the way. Shotgun marriage they used to call it, but nowadays they don't even bother with a ring. We married in the church in Compton. It was before James Baxter's time there, and the vicar gave us a lecture about the foolishness of youth, and how we had sinned and so on. After a great deal of repenting on our parts, he married us before it showed too much. My parents were aghast, and Eustace's were none too happy, but the shame of an illegitimate child was too much for any of them to accept. Eustace did his duty, although he wasn't so sure about me.'

'But you've stayed together for a long time.'

'We're like old socks. You get used to each other, and in time, the idea of separation and someone else no longer appeals. But I became cold towards him after our son died, and Eustace is still a man; he needed an outlet, and although I wished he hadn't, I couldn't do much about it.'

'You could have been more willing,' Clare said.

'I couldn't. You wouldn't understand.'

Clare chose not to mention that she did.

'Coming back to when you knifed your husband, explain what happened,' Tremayne said.

'Eustace came into the house late. I could see what he'd been up to.'

'A woman?'

'Yes.'

'But Gloria's dead, so it couldn't have been her.'

'It wasn't, but he's got a fancy woman somewhere, not in Compton.'

'Did you accuse him over this woman?'

'I made some comment, but he called me a dried-up old prune. That's not like Eustace to say such things, but I suppose this woman of his told him to stand up to me. I saw red, not so difficult with me, as I have a temper that's easy to inflame.'

'You answered him back?'

'I brought up Gloria, and the fact that the two of them had been sleeping together up to her death.'

'He denied it?'

'He didn't say much, just stood there with an inanimate face, as though butter wouldn't melt in his mouth. I struck him in the stomach, not that it hurt him, but he responded and slapped me across the face. I called him a son of a bitch, the devil's spawn.'

'And?'

'He grabbed me by the shoulders and shook me, accused me of all sorts of things, and how our son would still have been alive if it hadn't been for my nagging. That's when I grabbed the knife and tried to attack him.'

'There was no sign of blood in the house,' Clare said.

'Eustace, sensing the situation was bleak, made for the door. By then, my anger knew no limit. I continued after him and found him around the back of the barn. He saw me and attempted to get away, but I'm faster, and I rammed the knife into his back.'

'And afterwards?'

'I'm not sure. I hadn't meant to do it, and I didn't want him dead. By the time you arrived, I was still angry with Eustace, and I was pleased with what I had done. Now I've had time to reflect, and it was all my fault.'

'A judge could be swayed,' Tremayne said, 'but is it the truth?'

'What do you mean?'

'Did you have proof of Eustace and Gloria, and why did he kill her? How do you know that he did?'

'I was wrong, just angry. I know that she still liked him, that's all. I don't know who killed Gloria.'

***

Desdemona Foster sat in the front room of her house. Her husband sat on a chair opposite. Neither spoke, except to say the minimum necessary. Hamish Foster could see in his wife's face the anguish that surged through her.

Hamish knew of her flawed personality, the ease with which she listened to others, allowing them to form her opinions. For the first few years, she'd listened to him, but now she didn't. Now she needed others with more direct messages, more polarised and controversial.

Gloria Wiggins had been a firebrand and an opinionated woman, and Desdemona had worshipped her, but she was dead. Sheila Blatchford was not of the same calibre, but she held control of Desdemona, and now Margaret Wilmot did, but she was not as severe as the other two.

Desdemona Foster was back where her husband wanted her to be, under his loving care, listening to what he had to say, accepting his wisdom, but he knew it was not enough for her. She was a weak woman, not educated enough or dynamic enough to take control of her own views. Hamish knew that he did not have the mental strength that she wanted. He was a man who accepted a person for themselves, and the revelation about Margaret and Rupert did not concern him, nor the fact that Gladys Upminster had tried to kill Eustace. To him, all the events of the village were just the flotsam of life, and as long as he and Desdemona were not affected, then all was fine with him.

He looked over at his wife, saw the loveliness in her, the love he felt. No children had blessed their lives, not that Desdemona ever commented on her disappointment, and apart from a dog in the early years of their marriage, it had just been the two of them and the farm.

'None of it is important,' Hamish said, knowing full well that his comments would fall on deaf ears.

'But Margaret and Rupert Baxter. Why would she be with him? She's always such a sensible woman,' Desdemona replied. The usual decorative clothing had been replaced by a pink dressing gown to keep warm. An electric heater, the type with fake flames, attempted to warm the room, but it was large, the same as the rest of the house. Ideal in summer, but in winter it was impossible to heat. Money was not the issue in the Fosters' house, but Hamish was a frugal man, not given to waste when it was not needed, and the cold was transitory and could be overcome with appropriate clothing. Desdemona, a slight woman, felt the cold more than her husband, a man who carried more weight than he should.

'But why concern yourself? I can't say that I like Margaret very much, but it's none of our business if she wants to take Rupert as her lover. Look what's happened over at the Upminsters'. Gladys is with the police, Eustace is in hospital.'

'I knew about him,' Desdemona said.

'Knew what?'

'That he had another woman. Margaret told me the other day before I found out about her. What a thing to admit to. I'm glad we're not like that.'

Hamish felt inclined to go over to his wife and give her a hug but did not.

'How did Margaret know and why did she tell you?'

'Don't you realise that there are not many of us left now? Only four or five, and one of us is a murderer.'

'It's not us, and I can't see Margaret killing anyone. I always suspect the Woodcocks, but Barry's harmless and Gwen's devoted to her children.'

'I'm next,' Desdemona said.

'Why?'

'I can sense it.'

'But why you? You've done nothing wrong, never spoken out of turn.'

'I listened to Gloria and then Sheila. I don't think I can listen to Margaret anymore, not after what she has done.'

'Then will you listen to me?' Hamish said.

'You only say what I want to hear, not what I need to hear. They were my support, you're my love. Can't you accept it that way?'

Hamish Foster knew that as much as he loved his wife, she was a weak and easily led woman. He wondered if others had been coerced to commit acts that were unlawful and violent. He was concerned that his wife could be a murderer, and with the advice of others had rationalised it to be of no importance, whereas a single woman and a single man cohabiting was a punishable sin. He was a worried man.

Chapter 21

Gwyneth Wiggins, the second wife of Cuthbert Wiggins, was a roly-poly woman, as round as she was tall. She was the one person who hadn't been interviewed so far. Her husband, the person who had rendered Clare unconscious, was on bail on his own surety. He had been cleared of the murder of Stephanie Underwood and was at home with his wife when Tremayne and Clare knocked on the door.

A nondescript terrace house in a nondescript street, it was identifiable by the trimmed hedge at the front, the newly mown lawn. On one side, an unpainted house, a motorcycle in bits on the grass; on the other, an identical house painted an odd shade of grey.

'They suspended me from the bank pending the trial,' Wiggins said as he opened the door. Inside, the house was the same as it had been outside: spotless and well-presented. 'That's Gwyneth. Tidy house, tidy mind, that's her motto.'

'It's a credit to your wife. Yours must be the best in the street,' Clare said.

'Over-capitalised. I should know better as a bank manager, but I indulge my wife, not that she doesn't deserve it. I hope you're better. I'm still sorry about what happened.'

'So am I.'

'We'd like to speak to your wife,' Tremayne said.

'She's waiting for you. She knows about Gloria and Stephanie and what I did to your sergeant. She's not happy about it, but she's forgiven me, and she does understand.'

'Why you were in Compton?'

'Oh, yes. We've no secrets, that's how you stay married.'

Regardless of what had occurred, Clare had to admit to a liking for the man.

In the other room, Gwyneth Wiggins had prepared sandwiches and tea. Her husband stayed long enough to take a sandwich.

'You'll want to talk to Gwyneth without me, is that correct?' Cuthbert said as he left by the back door.

Before either Tremayne or Clare could respond, he was on the other side of the door and heading to a garden chair, near enough to be seen, far enough away so that he wouldn't hear the interview with his wife.

'Another cup?' Gwyneth said. She was a hospitable woman who apparently enjoyed having people over.

'Your children?'

'They'll not bother us.'

'Mrs Wiggins, you're aware why we're here?' Tremayne said.

'My Cuthbert wouldn't hurt a fly, and what I've heard of Gloria, she wasn't a good woman.'

'We never met her, not when she was alive,' Clare said.

'Cuthbert's still sorry for what he did to you.'

'I know, and he's still answerable for the assault and for leaving a murder scene. What has your husband told you?'

'He wanted to find Gloria's will. If she had not changed the original, then he's entitled to her estate. She mistreated him, and for many years he never looked at another woman. But then I came along, not as fat as you see me now, and he fell for me, I fell for him.'

'You're not fat, Mrs Wiggins,' Clare said.

'Well-rounded then.'

'As you say. Why wouldn't Gloria have changed her will? It's been many years since they divorced, and she was a fastidious woman.'

'Cuthbert thought she may have overlooked it. She cleaned him out, and we've survived, but not as well as we should.'

'Your house is a credit to you.'

'The area's not. With some of Gloria's money, it would make a difference. We could probably move somewhere else, but now Cuthbert's job is on the line. Even if he's acquitted, or held over for community service or something, his chances of keeping his job are slim, and there's no chance of promotion. Unfortunately, we're not in a good place at the present moment. Although we've got each other and the children. I suppose we can't have everything.'

'Not everything, but Mrs Wiggins, the truth. Have you been to Compton?'

'We drove through once many years ago. Cuthbert wanted to show me where his money was, although we never saw anyone. Or at least no one of importance, and certainly not Gloria. A couple were walking down the road, but my husband didn't know who they were, and they took no notice of us.'

'The cottage where Gloria lived, did you take any notice of it, detailed notice I mean?'

'It was a quick in and out of the village. I saw the front gate, the roof of the house, but not much else.'

'It's unusual for the second wife to see where the first wife lived.'

'I'm not the jealous type, and Cuthbert wanted me to know in case he wasn't around.'

'What do you mean?'

'If Cuthbert had passed on, then I was to keep a look out for any mention of Gloria. He told me about the will, and he had a certified copy. He knew it was a long shot, but anything to make my life better, that was Cuthbert. Always thinking of others, not himself.'

'Commendable, no doubt,' Tremayne said scathingly. He had a problem with people who just seemed too good, and Cuthbert Wiggins was being painted as a saint, and his wife, Gwyneth, as the loyal disciple.

'Mrs Wiggins, the problem we have is that we are short on suspects for the murder of Gloria Wiggins and others,' Clare said. 'It's clear that the other murders don't appear to have any connection to your husband, but Gloria's does.'

'I don't understand.'

'Gloria Wiggins' premature death is advantageous to you and your husband. Our concern is that he precipitated it.'

'It may be a godsend, but Cuthbert did not kill her.'

'No will has been found. It appears that your inheritance is intact.'

'Cuthbert's pleased that eventually he'll receive satisfaction for what she did to him, but we're not murderers.'

Outside the house, Tremayne lit up a cigarette. Clare looked around the area. 'Did you believe her?' she said.

'She puts on a brave face, but she must hate living with her neighbours. Check out her background, just in case.'

***

Eustace Upminster was discharged from hospital after six days and went to stay with Gladys's sister in Salisbury. He was anxious to have his wife by his side, but bail had been refused. Her lawyer had put forward an impassioned plea for leniency, as well as her husband's statement that it was a misunderstanding, which was read out at the hearing. However, Tremayne had been present at the hearing, and said that he regarded her as unpredictable.

In the end, Gladys Upminster was transferred to a minimum-security women's prison to await a full trial. Eustace Upminster was adamant that she would be back with him as soon as possible.

Events in the village moved forward at their slow and measured pace. The meetings continued at the pub, with Margaret Wilmot holding court; Desdemona Foster did not sit as close as she had before. A palpable air of distrust had settled over the bar, so much so that the next time Tremayne and Clare visited, they could sense it. If it hadn't been Compton and a murder enquiry, they would have gone somewhere else.

The Reverend Tichborne was also in jail, with his trial due in the next two months. His guilt seemed inevitable; his motive still debatable. Any attempt to obtain the necessary permissions to exhume his wife for further examination had been put on hold.

Hamish Foster sat in the pub, keeping a close watch on his wife. The Fosters, unlike in stature, reminded Tremayne of a nursery rhyme that his mother used to recite:

> *Jack Sprat could eat no fat.*
> *His wife could eat no lean.*
> *And so between the two of them,*
> *They licked the platter clean.*

With the Fosters, though, the position of husband and wife was reversed. Desdemona was small with an almost childlike body; her husband robust, the sort of man who'd eat a large steak at one sitting and then come back for more. The affection between the two was noticeable, although Desdemona listened to Margaret speak. The woman had a commanding voice with an air of authority, a sergeant-major's voice, Tremayne thought, although Margaret Wilmot would have considered herself a commissioned officer, not an NCO.

Rupert Baxter toiled behind the bar arranging bottles here and there, fiddling with the cash register, checking that the pumps for the beer on tap were primed. A general malaise existed, with no one saying more than necessary.

Barry and Gwen Woodcock came in through the door. Gwen looked over at Margaret and smiled; Barry headed for Baxter and a pint of beer.

'What's it with your wife and Margaret?' Tremayne said after Barry had propped himself up on a stool close to the bar.

'Complex. It would take time to tell you the story.'

'I've got the time. Why does Margaret hate you? Why haven't you told us before? We thought there was an animosity between the two women, but that's not the case. The issue is you.'

'Someone in here is a murderer, aren't they?' Barry said.

'That's what we believe. Eustace and Gladys Upminster could be the murderers. What's the truth about them?'

'There's not that much to tell you. Eustace's a good man, always has been, and Gladys was always easy to get on with. But their lives have been troubled, and now they're separated. They won't like that.'

'Gladys should have thought about that before she knifed her husband.'

'Can't you just say it was an accident and let bygones be bygones.'

'That's not how the law works. Gladys admitted to the crime, even said that Eustace was conducting an adulterous affair with Gloria. What do you reckon? True or false?'

'Eustace wouldn't have been near her, although he used to meet up with a woman two villages from here.'

'Since their son died?'

'It's been going on for years. I only know because I'm sometimes over there, and I've seen him on more than a few occasions. A decent-looking woman.'

'Why haven't you told us this before?'

'There was no reason to cause trouble.'

'She's known for some time, not that she liked it, but she accepted the status quo.'

'Any chance that Eustace's girlfriend is involved?'

'It seems unlikely, and what would she have to do with this village?'

'No harm in checking,' Barry said as he thrust his empty glass in front of Tremayne.

'Three pints of beer, one for yourself,' Tremayne said to Baxter.

'He's right about Gloria. There's no way that she was involved with Eustace. I'm not so sure about her apart from that, but she's been platonic in this village. If Eustace has been putting it about, it wasn't in Compton, and Gladys may have stabbed him, but she's a disturbed woman. You can't lock her up in jail for that.'

'We're conducting psychiatric tests to determine whether the woman is fit to stand trial or whether she should be confined to an institution until she's deemed fit to return to society.'

'Let her back with Eustace. We'll make sure that no harm comes to either of them.'

'You didn't do such a good job before,' Tremayne said.

'We weren't looking. Now we'll be more vigilant.'

'You should all be concerned as to who's next.'

'Do you think there'll be more?' Woodcock said. He had downed the last pint that Tremayne had purchased for him in record time. His conversation came at a cost.

Tremayne looked over at Clare, gave her a nod:
time to move on.

'The name of this woman? Tremayne said to
Woodcock.

'Linda Wilson. The first house on the left as you
enter the village. It's white, two-storey. There's a fountain
in the garden at the front.'

***

Two villages away, the village of Fitzhampton. Not the
bleakness of Compton with its post-war architecture, its
red-brick cottages, where the only buildings of some
appeal were the pub and the church. Fitzhampton was
thatched cottages and a stream flowing through the
centre, ducks swimming, a couple of youths with fishing
rods. Realising that they had missed the house, Clare
turned the car around and headed back towards
Compton.

'Over there,' Tremayne said.

'I was looking for something more modest,' Clare
had to admit.

On the high side of the road, and behind a solid
fence, stood a detached house of exquisite beauty.

'It must be two to three hundred years old,'
Tremayne said.

'Georgian possibly, although it could have been
built later.'

Clare parked the car, and the two of them walked
up the path. On the front door, a large brass knocker.
Tremayne used the knocker as well as a bell to the side.
After five minutes, the door opened. A woman in her
mid-forties, elegantly dressed, stood before them.

'I expected you to turn up at some time,' she said.

Tremayne and Clare showed their warrant cards, the woman checking them in detail.

'Come in, please. Make yourselves comfortable. I won't be long, and then you can have my undivided attention.'

The two police officers looked around where they were sitting. On the walls, paintings and posters, the furniture a combination of contemporary and antique. The room, as did the house, oozed affluence, yet the woman who had opened the door had had a mischievous look about her as if she somehow did not belong.

After what seemed an eternity, Linda Wilson reappeared. 'Sorry about that, but you can't hurry these things.'

'What things are that? Clare asked.

'We'll come back to that later. Is this about Eustace?'

'It is,' Tremayne said.

'Dear Eustace, one of my regulars.'

'Regular what?'

Clare thought that Tremayne was obtuse in asking.

'Client. I've got bills to pay the same as everyone else.'

'Prostitution?'

'Nothing as sordid as that. Lonely men that I approve of, and can afford their time with me. I've known Eustace for years, and he comes over every few weeks for a few hours. We're discreet, although everyone in the village must know, not that I care.'

'You're an escort?' Tremayne said.

'High-class, and sometimes I'm here, sometimes I'm overseas. Eustace is an exception in that he's not as wealthy as the others, but I genuinely like the man, not so much the others, not always.'

'This house?'

'It belongs to a benefactor, although he doesn't come here, and please, don't ask his name. I won't tell you, confidentiality is paramount.'

'Like a doctor,' Clare said.

'That's what I am, a healer. I've no shame about it, although if you weren't the police, we wouldn't be discussing the matter.'

'Your relationship with the other people in the village?'

'Some won't talk to me, but most will. A scarlet woman adds allure to the village, and my being here gives them an edginess to their lives. Some of the women probably envy me, and their husbands often try out their charms on me.'

'Any success?'

'Not on your own doorstep, isn't that the saying?'

'Something like that,' Clare said.

Both Tremayne and Clare warmed to the woman and her stark honesty. It was not for them to pass moral judgement, only to find out how she tied in with Eustace Upminster and his wife, and if she knew the others that had died in Compton.

'Were you shocked by what happened to Eustace?'

'Yes, I was. I know that Gladys had become strange after her son died, but attempting to kill Eustace came as a shock. I phoned the hospital, they told me he was going to survive.'

'He's been discharged. He's more concerned about Gladys than himself.'

'That's Eustace. He was always devoted to her, more so than to me.'

'It's clear that you've known Eustace for a long time,' Tremayne said. 'It may be best if you explain how.'

'Call me Linda. No doubt you could both do with a cup of tea.'

'We could,' Tremayne said.

After a few minutes, the interview resumed.

'I grew up in the area, the childhood friend of Gladys's younger sister. There's a fifteen-year age gap between the sisters. I've known Gladys from back then, and then Eustace. I was sixteen, precocious and well-developed for my age. Eustace was married to Gladys by then, and it was a rough patch for them. Most married people have rough patches, not that I'd know, not from personal experience, that is. One night, we were alone somewhere or the other, and we ended up in bed together. It didn't seem to worry either of us, and there was no guilt. I fell for him, but he wasn't interested in me, not as a long-term proposition, and besides, he had Gladys. He was right, of course. I wasn't the sort of a person to settle for one man and one place. I was ambitious, wanting to see the world, wanting to be rich. We met up a few times over the next couple of months, and then I left the area, went overseas. Eventually, I came back to the area, an attempt to re-establish my roots, an attempt at normalcy.

'I met Eustace in Salisbury one day some years back, and our casual get-togethers continued, interspersed with my other obligations.'

'Eustace is not a client?'

'Not with me. He's my tenuous hold on what could have been a normal life, but now, with Gladys in prison and Eustace almost killed, it may present a complication.'

'It won't,' Clare said. 'He intends to stand by her.'

'Miss Wilson, does your relationship with Eustace Upminster have any bearing on the murders in Compton?' Tremayne asked.

'Gladys knew about me, although I've not spoken to her for many years. Certainly not in the last twenty. I don't think she was ever an affectionate woman, always a little sullen, but Eustace needed her, not me. Eustace is a tactile man, but he needs a strong person to control him. Gladys was that person. And if she's in prison, he'll be there every day doing what he can to make her life more comfortable.'

'This house?'

'As I said, a benefactor.'

'Have you been to Compton in the last few years?'

'When I was younger, but I preferred the bright lights of London back then. Apart from Eustace and Gladys, I don't know anyone else in Compton apart from those I know from my school days. Of those that died, I vaguely recollect meeting Gloria Wiggins.'

An interesting interlude in the murder investigations, Tremayne would have admitted, but not a lot had been gained by meeting Linda Wilson. Unless advice and investigation to the contrary revealed otherwise, she was just a minor player, and not involved. Clare intended to do some research on the good-natured and vivacious woman who purveyed her body to men of wealth with no moral compunction.

Chapter 22

A lull in the murder count in Compton, not that there were many of the core group left alive, gave Tremayne time to reflect. He had to admit to himself that he felt a weariness in his body and that he walked slower than before. There was a time when he could have worked from dawn to dusk and often much later, then downed more than his fair share of pints of beer at the pub, and then repeated the process day in, day out. But now, any attempt to emulate that meant a stay in the hospital to recuperate, a berating from Jean and accusing glances from Yarwood. He determined that the next offer from Superintendent Moulton would be met more receptively than previously.

Tremayne knew it was not what he wanted as he had been a policeman all of his adult life, from when he had been a cadet up to inspector, and it had been a vocation, not a nine-to-five ordeal. He knew that retirement would not be endless rounds of golf, or pottering in the garden, both of which left him cold, but an inevitable decline to nothingness. He was not a happy man the day after meeting Linda Wilson.

Tremayne and Clare were in the office, a rare occurrence in the middle of the day. Outside the rain was torrential and it made driving difficult and policing almost impossible. At least Tremayne's idea of policing. Clare could still continue to work, her laptop indispensable, and at night in her bed, she had an iPad and a cat for company.

She had phoned Doctor Warner the previous night, the doctor who had told Tremayne to ease up or it'd be an early grave for him. The relationship between the police sergeant and the doctor was back on, but whether it would last or not, Clare did not know, only that occasionally the cat was not sufficient in her bed.

Doctor Warner qualified as he was enamoured of her, having professed love on more than one occasion, a feeling she could not reciprocate. She felt a fondness for him, but it wasn't love. That was reserved for Harry Holchester, but he was long dead and buried.

Even though it had been two in the morning, the previous night she had felt the irresistible urge to visit his grave in the village of Avon Hill. Apart from the rustling of the leaves in the trees to one side of the churchyard, a light in the upstairs window of the rectory and the hooting of an owl, it was just her and Harry, his grave still tended by some of the locals. She placed some flowers that she had had in a vase at her cottage and stood there with just the light from her iPhone.

There had been many attempts at closure after Harry had died violently, and even though she hadn't visited his grave in over six months, the bond still existed. She determined that this would be the last time, knowing full well that it wouldn't be. Clare had walked away from the grave, sobbing profusely, but she would still see the doctor, and if he wanted to share her bed, then he would be welcomed.

'You're not your usual irascible self,' Clare said to Tremayne in his office.

'New Year's resolution,' Tremayne replied.

'It's not the new year, and you're not into resolutions.'

'The inevitable passing of time. A reflection of what I've achieved in life.'

'The premise of an old man, and you aren't old yet. You're still the best police officer at Bemerton Road Police Station.'

'That may be the case, but my time is drawing to a close. Even if I delay Moulton, there are only a few more years before my retirement is mandatory. I can't stop the ticking of the clock, any more than you can.'

Clare knew what he meant. Her biological clock was ticking, faster than ever, and the need to have a child persisted. 'It's no use worrying about it,' she said.

'The occasional twinge, the ache in the knees, the sore back. It's not something I can stop, only ignore. Jean would want me to be with her so that she could fuss, but if I were there every day, I'd drive her mad.'

'Tell her, see what can be done to alleviate the conditions. Who knows, medicine may help.'

'Enough of the heart-to-heart,' Tremayne said, reverting to type. 'What did you find out about Linda Wilson?'

'Her story checks out. She was a friend of Gladys's younger sister. I even found a school photo of the two of them when they were eleven, and then another when they were sixteen. Linda Wilson was, as she said, well-endowed, and not afraid to show it. There's a history of promiscuity, and she has been to Compton more than a few times. Even a photo of her with Gladys, although it's a dated photo.'

'Where did you find that?'

'Instagram. Linda's an avid user of social media.'

'I liked the woman,' Tremayne said.

'I thought you did.'

'Not in that way. She had a refreshing honesty about her, something sadly lacking in Compton. Any black marks against her?'

'None that I can see. She's obviously well-travelled, her trips overseas show that, and her story about Eustace holds up, although he would have been in his thirties when she was sixteen. She was over the age of consent, but only just. However, a thirty-one-year-old man and a sixteen-year-old woman, even if she looked older, would not have been readily accepted by most people. We need to check who knew and if it's relevant.'

'Would it be?'

'Do you have any better ideas? We're running out of potential murderers. We could do with a few more, and Linda, regardless of how refreshing she was, is suspect, and she must have been around some unsavoury characters over the years. No doubt she picked up a tip or two on dishonesty, criminal intent, even murder.'

***

Rupert Baxter stood knee-deep in the river. He was wearing waders as he flicked his fishing rod, the hook landing in the same area every time. It was one of the few times when he was at peace with the world; one of the few times when his prodigious mind stopped to rest. He had seen the fish that he was after on a few occasions and had even snagged it once, only for it to drop off his hook as he had tried to wrestle it to the shore. He was determined that day to succeed, having seen it swimming through the reeds not far from where he was standing. The fish, Baxter was sure, was smarter than it looked, the fish equivalent of him in intellect. It was a battle between two minds, and if he caught it, it wouldn't be tasty, and Baxter knew that he would not deprive the fish of its life.

On the shore, a couple of people wandered by. They were not locals, and Baxter took no notice of them, only to give them a cursory nod of the head. One of the onlookers reciprocated but spoke no words. They moved on, leaving Baxter to his fish and his peace.

A fish broke the surface of the river not far from where the elusive fish lurked. Up above, the sky was clear, and the temperature on the shore was crisp, while in the water it was even colder. Baxter knew that he would devote another thirty minutes to the fish, and then declare it the victor that day.

The events at the Upminsters' farm had raised the tension in the village, and the night before he had argued with Margaret, after telling her who it was who had committed the murders and why. And now, she was back at her manor house, and he wasn't sure what she would do, what he should do. The police would be interested in his analysis, no doubt claim it for their own, not that it concerned him. If he had wanted fame and recognition for his unique approach to quantum physics, he would have been out on the lecture circuit, receiving awards, and being paid well. His papers had been published, and although there had been some who had visited the pub to discourse on his area of research, not many had come in total. He cast his line one more time, knowing that his mind was not at one with the fish.

'Another day we will meet on the battlefield of life,' he said. He had to admit that the fish had a better life than him; it did not have to deal with the reality of revealing the truth.

***

Linda Wilson had remained unflappable during the visit of the two police officers. But isn't that what I'm meant to do, she thought. To pretend that I'm comfortable when I'm not, especially with that thug in the Greek Islands, and how about that banker, stiff upper lip, well-respected in the city, yet a pervert. How I hated him.

The visit of Inspector Tremayne and Sergeant Yarwood had left her perplexed and a little frightened. She had loved Eustace when she had been in her teens, an innocent love.

She remembered the first time she had sold herself. A former boss, who had propositioned her, had taken her to a hotel in the countryside for the weekend. 'I'll set you up in a flat in Mayfair, pay your expenses,' he had said as they had driven along in his Porsche with the hood down.

She hadn't wanted to, the man was not the most attractive, but he was decent, and eventually she had agreed. With time, she got used to the generosity of a man in return for the comforts of life, and what she had to give in return concerned her less, but the return to Salisbury had given her time for reflection.

She'd been six months in Fitzhampton when she had seen Eustace walking casually through the centre of Salisbury. It was another month before he shared her bed again. He was her first love, a forbidden love as he was married, and she had never forgotten.

It had also been a time for him to unburden himself to her, and later to tell her about how cold Gladys had become after their son died, the inconsolable grief that she felt. He also told her about the village of Compton and the various personalities, and how he hated the place, but couldn't leave it.

And now, Eustace had been knifed by Gladys, and Linda knew that she wanted to see him. She drove to the same house where they had made love many years before, and where Gladys's sister, Mary, now resided in the home of her parents. Linda knew she would not be welcome.

'You've got a nerve,' Mary said. She was the same age as Linda, yet she looked much older, the result of three children, and if the truth was known, a husband who used to beat her until he had walked out three years earlier, never to be heard from again. Mary hoped that he would never return, and in his absence, she had filed for divorce, the house belonging solely to her. It had been given by their parents to both Gladys and Mary, but Gladys had signed over her half out of love for a sister, and an understanding of the strain that the woman had been living under.

Not only had the husband been of little worth, the eldest son was a delinquent, the daughter, not yet sixteen, a tart, and the youngest son not entirely right in the head and a simpleton.

And there she was, Linda Wilson, the nemesis, Mary's one-time friend.

'I'm sorry, Mary,' Linda said. 'I just had to know that Eustace was fine.'

'He's fine, no thanks to you.'

'I'm innocent, Mary. I'd like to see him.'

The door opened, bringing a remembrance of what had been before that awful night so many years ago when Gladys had found Eustace and Linda in bed together. The accusations that flew, the pulling of Linda's hair, the harsh words said by Linda in return.

And in time, the recriminations and Gladys leaving Eustace once again for a couple of months, driving her parents mad after she had returned to the parental home, a young and unruly child in tow.

And now, the woman who had caused such conflict was at the door. The two women embraced.

'Your life has been different to mine,' Mary said as she wiped a tear from her eye.

'Some good, some bad, but I've missed you.'

'I've seen you in Salisbury, but you wouldn't have recognised me.'

'I had, but what could I say? I never wanted to hurt Gladys or you, but these things happen.'

'Gladys said you were selling yourself.'

'Does it bother you?'

'It would have to be better than the drudgery that I've endured over the years. My husband was a bastard.'

'Eustace told me that you had had it rough. I could have helped.'

'Even if I wanted it, you couldn't have. And besides, money's not the issue.'

Inside the house, Eustace sat in a wheelchair. He looked up as Linda entered, wanted to dash over and give her a hug, not out of love, but out of friendship. A person who had visited him, but not to criticise, as Mary had done, for his treatment of Gladys, not that he had done anything wrong. Or the police continually quizzing him, attempting to find out a reason for Gladys attacking him.

'Thanks for coming,' Eustace said.

'I wasn't sure, but then the police visited me.'

'There's nothing to be ashamed of, and even Mary, not that she'd approve openly, would understand. You two were such great friends once.'

'Before that day, but let's not dwell on the past.'

'I'll heal, but it's Gladys I'm worried about. I want to go and see her.'

'Why don't you?'

'Mary doesn't have a car, and I don't want to ask anyone else.'

'We'll go now. My car's outside, and you don't have to tell Gladys that I brought you.'

Chapter 23

Barry Woodcock had his head under the bonnet of his old Land Rover; his wife, Gwen, was in the farmhouse kitchen baking a cake, while the three children, usually not visible, were scurrying around the place. One of them was throwing a ball to a dog, another sat on the step leading up to the front door reading a book, and the third crawled along the porch. The farm had an air of tranquillity. However, disturbing news had been received from Forensics about a hitherto unresolved piece of evidence from outside Gloria Wiggins' garage, a plant leaf that had been found squashed into the mud. It had taken several weeks, and in the end Louise Regan, Forensics head, had driven to the Royal Botanic Gardens in London for one of their experts to identify the leaf. It belonged to a Crested Cow-wheat, a small flower rarely found in England. And now, the complication was that at the far end of the Woodcocks' farm, the plant had been found growing. It wasn't damning evidence, as the area where the plant grew was not isolated. A path ran alongside, only separated from it by a low fence, but no one would have stooped to pick up the rare plant, as it was not attractive, no more than a weed to the uninformed.

'Barry, we need a serious word,' Tremayne said. Clare thought the three children were attractive: the eldest already starting to look like his father with the high forehead, the prominent chin. The daughter had the look of her mother, the eyes of her father, while the youngest showed no visible signs of either parent, but it was mainly face down on the floor. Clare thought the floor too cold to be crawling over, but then she was no expert on the subject.

'Two minutes,' Barry said.

After ten minutes, not the two stated, Woodcock came into the house and sat at the kitchen table with Tremayne and Clare. 'That's the problem with old vehicles,' he said. 'It's not a lot of money to repair, but it's time. I'll have to take off the head, check the valves, and then replace the head gasket. There goes my Sunday.'

'How are you with pulleys, Barry?' Tremayne said.

'What's this all about?'

'A leaf was found up at Gloria's garage. We believe that it came in with her murderer.'

'A leaf? What's that to do with me?'

'It's rare, and your farm has some of it in the far corner, next to the path. We can prove it came from there, and it's not as if other people have trodden around your farm.'

'Nobody except Gwen and me, and she'd not go up there often.'

'The leaf connects the murder scene and your farm.'

'I don't know why. It's not as if I go traipsing around the fields. There are some cattle over that way, and I sometimes go up there in the winter to give them some feed, but not recently.'

'What's the story with the path alongside?'

'It's just one of those public thoroughfares that have been there for hundreds of years. We sometimes go for a walk up it on a Sunday, Gwen and me and the children. Also, hikers use it on a regular basis. You can walk almost into Salisbury on the paths. But why would anyone pick up a plant, it makes no sense?'

'The facts point to someone walking on the plant without realising what it was, or picking it up.'

'The cows could have carried it into the yard, and then dropped it,' Barry said.

Tremayne wasn't sure what to make of what the man was saying. Woodcock had an air of bewildered innocence about him, and others had said that he was not too bright. Yet Rupert Baxter portrayed the jovial publican with great conviction, and he had admitted to a searing intellect. Was Barry Woodcock more than he seemed? Tremayne did not know. The man's educational qualifications had shown that he had left school with no O or A levels, and since then his life had been on the farm.

Lacking any more questions, Tremayne and Clare left the farmhouse with Barry and walked across the field to where the leaf had come from.

'I don't know much about horticulture,' Tremayne said as the three of them stood looking down at where the plant grew.

'It's a weed to me,' Woodcock said. 'No idea why the cows haven't eaten it. Maybe it doesn't taste good, although I've not found them to be fussy with what they chew on. The grass in summer, a bale of hay in the winter.'

On another side of the field, the cows grazed without taking any notice of the three people.

'It gets cold up close to the trees on the other side of the field,' Woodcock said.

'Perishing cold,' Tremayne agreed. 'Now look here, Woodcock. We've gone out of our way to give you the benefit of the doubt, but each time the evidence mounts against you. Nothing concrete, you'll understand, but circumstantially you're guilty. A couple of hundred years ago, you'd be convicted and strung up for less, but nowadays we'll not get a conviction, though we can hold you pending further investigations.'

'I can't be away from the farm. There's too much to do.'

'We're trusting you on this one, but each time we come out here, another titbit becomes known. What do you know about Eustace and this other woman?'

'We all knew, not that we ever spoke to him about it, and Gwen wouldn't have told Gladys.'

'We're not sure if she knew the extent of the affair, but she had apparently accepted it.'

'If I did something like that, Gwen wouldn't stay calm.'

'Violent?'

'She's got a temper, and maybe she'd hit me, but it's not going to happen, is it?'

'How would we know,' Tremayne said.

'I wouldn't do that, not to Gwen. We're too close for that, and besides, Eustace may have needed the other woman, but with Gwen, I don't.'

'A good marriage?' Clare asked. The three had moved away from the far side of the field and were back in the farmyard.

'I reckon so. The Upminsters' marriage was always fiery, not that we ever saw it, but sometimes Eustace would have a black eye. The Fosters rarely argue, and you know Desdemona.'

'We've still not figured her out,' Clare said.

'Nobody has,' Woodcock said. 'She's a local, the same as we all are, but she doesn't look as though she comes from farming stock. Her father was a short man, wiry, with red hair. Desdemona takes after him, but she's got no strength to her, not like he did. He'd be out on his farm day in, day out, and still be in the pub three times a week for a few pints. Desdemona, even when she was at school and then as a teenager, didn't socialise much, and she was not out and about with the local lads. More of a stay-at-home, not like Hamish.'

'Hamish is local, we know that.'

'Local, he certainly is. Anyway, he used to get out and about, and then he was with Desdemona. Not sure what he saw in her at the time, although she was attractive, more demure than the others and he fell hook, line, and sinker for her.'

'Another dead end,' Tremayne wryly admitted to Clare as they left the farm, with Barry Woodcock looking at them less than enthusiastically. He still had five hours more work for the day, and it was late afternoon. It would be dark, and the children would be in bed, before he entered the farmhouse that night.

If Tremayne and Clare were psychic, they would have known that he was a worried man. However, Woodcock soon put the thoughts of impending doom to one side and headed back to the field to bring in the cows for milking. Then he had to cut some firewood to heat the house, let alone clean out the barn, and as for the Land Rover, that would be a job for another day.

***

Cuthbert Wiggins sat on the stool that Tremayne usually took in the bar at Rupert Baxter's pub. It had been two days since Barry and Gwen Woodcock had been interviewed at their farm, and Tremayne and Clare had spent most of the time at the police station. Not that Tremayne enjoyed his time there, but there was paperwork to deal with, the prosecution cases of the Reverend Tichborne and Gladys Upminster to be dealt with, the key performance indicators that needed addressing for Superintendent Moulton, and a chance for Tremayne's aching knees to recuperate.

At Compton, a man who should not have been in the village, as one of the conditions of his bail had been to keep clear, spoke to Baxter. Wiggins had consumed his first pint and was ordering a second. 'Do you know who I am?'

'I've not seen you in here before,' Baxter said.

'I couldn't keep away. I'm in a lot of trouble, and the police are still suspicious of me.'

'There's only one person I can think of.'

'Cuthbert Wiggins, I'm pleased to make your acquaintance,' Wiggins said as he thrust his pudgy hand across the bar to shake that of Baxter's.

Baxter shook the man's hand firmly. 'We always thought you were a myth,' he said.

'That was how Gloria wanted it to be. I hadn't seen her for a long time before she died. Not that it's important, but what was she like as she aged?'

208

'Vindictive, venomous.' Baxter saw no reason to moderate his opinion purely on the basis that the man opposite had been married to the woman once.

'She didn't change.'

'Why are you here?' Baxter asked. He looked at the man opposite, could see that he was shorter than Gloria, yet she had married him when she had eschewed other men's advances. Rupert remembered that he had attempted to take her out on her return to the village, but she had not wanted him, and no man had been near her since then. And yet, a small, neatly dressed and bespectacled man had wedded and bedded the woman.

'I don't know. I came here not so long ago, and it didn't turn out well. It may be just an attempt to make amends, to convince those that knew her that I was real, and I didn't kill Stephanie.'

'You certainly hit the lovely Sergeant Yarwood heavily on the head.'

'I still regret that. Is she fine?'

'She appears to be. They're here most days, Tremayne and Yarwood.'

'They'll not like me being here.'

'Someone said you were after Gloria's last will and testament, hoping to benefit from it.'

'Not out of malice. She was a lovely woman when I met her, and then she dumped me, took me to the cleaners.'

'Don't they all,' Baxter said, remembering back to when his wife had moved out, the trouble he'd had afterwards, the costs, the emotional distress.

'I never fully understood what changed in her.'

'I knew her as a child, and there wasn't much affection in her. Sure, she had friends, and then boyfriends, but you never knew with Gloria what she was thinking. Her parents were the same. Did you ever meet them?'

'Briefly, and only the once.'

'Her father was a soulless man,' Baxter said. 'I don't think he ever smiled. Her mother would at least say hello and occasionally stop for a conversation, but she didn't smile either. Did you kill her?'

'Who? Gloria? Not me. I never saw her after the divorce, and I've never been to the village since then. Believe me, I wasn't that sad when she died. It seems heartless, but I can't say anything else.'

'No one here was distraught. A sense of disbelief but nothing else. Are you staying?'

'I shouldn't, but I feel drawn to the place. A premonition of something evil.'

'There's a room upstairs. Fifty pounds for the night, although you might have to deal with the ghost.'

'Is there one?'

'There are some that say there is, and I don't discourage the speculation, but no, there's nothing. Just creaking floorboards, and me winding my way up to the toilet during the night.'

'I'll take it. No doubt the police will be out here soon enough.'

'No doubt. Tremayne likes his pint of beer, and I serve the best.'

Chapter 24

Tremayne sat in the living room of his house; he was
feeling the worst he had felt for some time. If asked, he
would have said it was just the malaise of a murder
investigation that had stretched on for too long.

On the television, a movie of no great merit about
a lone hero righting wrongs, pining for a lost girlfriend,
finding solace in the arms of another. Tremayne flicked
the switch on the remote to off. Fiction may be
entertaining for the masses, but the taking of a life,
cavalier in the case of the lone hero, was neither romantic
nor necessary. To Tremayne, murder was a messy
business fuelled by anger and frustration and greed, not
by nobler reasons.

Tremayne looked over at Jean who was nursing a
stray cat she had found, and which had adopted the two
of them. The police inspector had to admit to an affinity
with the animal. It did not demand, it cared for itself, and
as long as it was fed, it gave affection in return, and it
didn't need walking. Tremayne stretched his right leg

which had previously been bent at an awkward angle. His knee jabbed, a grimace visible on his face.

'You're getting too old for long nights out in the cold,' Jean said. The man knew she was right, but he was not ready. It had been his first time in front of that television for some time, and it was clear that being invalided and confined to watching it every day, every night, would be anathema to him.

'I need a doctor,' he said. 'Someone who understands.'

'Someone who understands that a silly old fool prefers to be out hunting down villains instead of spending his days at home in a warm house.'

'It's not that. It's the inevitable transition from police officer to retired police officer, and then what?'

'We've all got to go sometime,' Jean said. 'No point collapsing on the job. There's no credit in that.'

Tremayne knew that Jean was right, and he had considered it, but not yet, and not while there were murders to solve. He got out of his chair, attempting not to show the pain, but Jean could see through him. She said nothing. She knew he was a cantankerous man, yet she still loved him, always had in her own way, even when she had been married to another, and he was on his own.

'I'll be thirty minutes,' Tremayne said.

'No doubt he'll have something for you, not that you're listening to me. We can survive financially now that I've sold my house.'

'I need another year. Once Yarwood's made up to inspector, then I'll call it quits. Okay?'

'Okay by me, but you'll come up with another excuse.'

'Not this time,' Tremayne said as he closed the front door behind him.

The doctor was sympathetic, a similar age to Tremayne. Society deemed them past it, but neither of them was ready, and a lifetime of experience with a fertile mind and a failing body suited neither. 'These will help, two a day,' the doctor said.

***

Clare kept in contact with Doctor Warner, an attempt to meet up soon for a weekend away, but he was not pushing, she could sense it. She was sure that his ardour had moderated and that he had been looking for someone who fitted the mould: someone who wanted a child, and weekends and nights together, and regular hours.

If that was the case, Clare realised that the weekend was off. She knew she'd have to pin him down before then, and they would have to meet somewhere neutral to thrash it out. She had to admit that either way she would not be upset.

As Clare pondered the doctor and Tremayne nursed his knee, out at Compton a man who should not have been there was making himself comfortable in his bed. He would not admit that the idea of a ghost scared him, due to his sensitive nature and a mother who had believed in such things.

Cuthbert Wiggins turned over in his bed and looked out of the small window, the panorama of the village laid out before him. Up high to one side, the cottages of Gloria and Stephanie, both dark and cold. On either side of them, lights blazed in the clear night. A mist was enveloping the valley. He realised that coming to Compton was a mistake and that no good would come of it, but he knew he could not leave. Gloria's house contained a secret, a secret that he believed he had solved.

213

He remembered her fastidiousness for keeping documents close to her and locked in a small metal box, and when they had lived together, it had been locked in a cupboard.

Wiggins rose from his bed, the floorboards creaking. He had intended to wait, but time was of the essence. He crept down the stairs, his pyjamas under his shirt and trousers, and wearing a heavy jacket to keep warm.

Downstairs, the pub was quiet and in darkness. He opened the back door and let himself out. Gloria's house was within walking distance, and he walked up the road, keeping to the shadows, careful to ensure that none of the lighted windows of the houses he passed had a person on the other side.

Wiggins halted outside Stephanie Underwood's house and for a moment felt sorrow at having seen her dead in that chair. He climbed over the low fence at the front of her house and walked around to the back. A small fence separated one cottage from the other. He cleared it quickly and walked, almost tip-toed, to the back door of Gloria's cottage, the crime scene tape visible across the door. Wiggins remembered her penchant for the security of her metal chest, but an ambivalence to locking the house, and her hiding a key near to a tree.

And now Wiggins had espied two likely candidates. He put his hands into the ground and ferreted around the base of one tree, before moving to the second.

'Voila,' he said, almost audibly, as his fingers felt the metallic object enclosed in a plastic bag.

Carefully pulling the crime scene tape on the door of the house to one side, he used the key and opened the door. Passing through the kitchen, he headed for the

214

main bedroom. It was clear that the police had been over the place, yet they hadn't known what they were looking for.

He had only wanted to talk to Stephanie Underwood, to find someone who may have been able to help him, but he had been too late. Now, in that bedroom, he could see what he was looking for. Two of the floorboards underneath the bed had a cut across them, the torch on his iPhone picking it up. He crept forward on all fours and inserted the blade of a knife into the cut; the boards moved. He eased them upwards to reveal a cavity; the metal chest was there. He removed it, taking time to ensure that nothing else was disturbed, even remembering to blow dust from one area to the next as he replaced the floorboards. As he left the cottage, he ensured that there was no sign of his visit. Outside the cottage, he closed the door, repositioned the crime scene tape, and put the key back where he had found it, making sure that the soil was compacted as it had been when he had first discovered it.

Wiggins retraced his steps to the pub. He was feeling elated. The metal chest, the same as he remembered, was no longer shiny and red. Now it was scratched and rusty, but when he shook it, the contents inside rustled. He knew that what he wanted lay close by, separated from him only by the lid and the lock.

He was too excited to sleep, too conscious of waking Baxter who might start asking questions. Wiggins lay on his bed and imagined how his life and that of his wife would change with the contents of the box. Even if it contained another will, what did it matter? No one would ever find it. He thanked Gloria for her obsession of not entrusting her documents to the safekeeping of a bank, even though she had worked in one, and for not registering another will. He knew that it was all going to work out.

Chapter 25

Cuthbert Wiggins left the pub at eight in the morning following his sojourn up to Gloria's cottage. He knew he couldn't wait to get home before opening the small metal box.

'No need to worry about breakfast,' he said to Baxter as he paid his money and left.

'It's full English.'

'Next time,' Wiggins said. He walked out to the pub's carpark and got into his car and drove away. Two hundred yards further up the road, he got out of the car and sat on a bench by the river. He took the box, and with his hands shaking, he inserted his knife into one edge of the lid and tried to pry it open. The blade was too weak and was bending as he levered. He looked around him, unable to find anything of use.

When I get home, he thought to himself. As he raised himself from the seat, a person was standing behind him.

'I saw you up at Gloria's last night,' a voice said.

'What do you mean?' Wiggins said as he looked around to see who it was, a clear view not possible due to the sun in his eyes.

'We don't like outsiders in Compton.'

This time Wiggins did not reply, his voice muted as the branch of a tree had been smashed across his head, causing him to tumble forward and into the river.

'A job well done' the voice said as its owner walked away, grasping the box.

Wiggins, a strong swimmer in his youth, and before the weight had come on, did not die that day. He was severely stunned, yet the cold of the water revived him sufficiently for him to swim to shore. On the far side of the river, two hundred yards from where he had involuntarily entered it, he lay on the bank. On the other side of the river he could see the pub.

'Help, help,' Wiggins shouted, although no sound emanated from his mouth. He realised that he did not have the energy to swim back to the other side of the river. He sat up, peeling the wet clothes from his body. He was shivering, and hypothermia was setting in. Outside the pub, the familiar figure of Rupert Baxter. Wiggins, with one herculean effort, lifted himself up by holding onto a tree and stood up. He raised his arms to wave, and with one final attempt shouted across to Baxter.

The man opposite looked Wiggins' way and came over to the river. 'What's happened?'

'I need help. I'm freezing.'

After being retrieved, Wiggins sat in the pub. An electric heater was on full, a hot drink in his hand. Fifteen minutes later, his condition stabilised. 'Someone hit me over the head.'

'Why?'

Wiggins was sure the truth would not be appreciated, and he said nothing. Baxter picked up his phone and dialled Tremayne. He told him to get out to Compton urgently.

Wiggins realised the situation was precarious. His retrieval of the metal box had been flawless, his departure without raising undue suspicion had worked, but now he was front and centre, and the police were on their way. He knew he needed out.

'I have to go,' Wiggins said, knowing that questions were about to be asked for which he had no answer.

Baxter realised that the police would have questions for him as well; namely, why he had not told them about Wiggins being in the village. Both of the men had reason to be concerned, and even though Baxter had phoned Tremayne now, it would only momentarily deflect further questions.

Margaret Wilmot came into the pub, took one look at Wiggins, and moved over to where Baxter stood. She slapped him hard across the face, catching the man off-guard and causing him to take one step back. 'You damn fool, Rupert. You were meant to keep a watch on him.'

'It was you that hit me,' Wiggins said, recognising Margaret's deep voice.

'You'd be dead if it were up to me,' she replied. 'You come in here causing trouble, stirring up a hornet's nest, and after I had it under control.'

'What do you mean?' Baxter said. He had seen a severe Margaret, a pious and sanctimonious Margaret, even a loving Margaret, but what he saw now was a departure from all three. This time Margaret was talking without due care and with anger.

'I saw that silly little man,' Margaret said. 'Last night while you were asleep or getting drunk, Wiggins left the pub and broke into Gloria's cottage. He found the box.'

'Of what use is it to you?' Wiggins said.

'Shut up, you little toad. I've not finished.' Margaret said. She turned to face Rupert. 'What do you think the police are going to say when they find you sitting down with Wiggins? They're going to put two and two together, and this time they might get it right.

'I could have died,' Wiggins said, hoping for sympathy.

'And good riddance. Oh, yes, I know all about you and Gloria, even where you live now, and how many children you have and that scruffy little bank that you manage.'

'Why?'

'It's my job to know what goes on in this village, and who's sleeping with who, who's cheating on their taxes, and why Gloria took your money.'

'It doesn't make sense to me,' Wiggins said.

'Not to me either,' Baxter said. 'What do you hope to achieve by all this? You're guilty of attempted murder, and I can't protect you. Wiggins is here, clearly concussed and still shivering. Tremayne's no dummy and that sergeant of his is sharp. They'll smell a rat if we come up with a lame-brained story.'

'Wiggins, you were after proof that there was not another will, correct?'

'Yes, nothing else. She owes me that.'

'She owes you nothing. I wanted something else. Keep quiet about what has happened to you and we have a deal. I'll give you a will if it's there. If it is, then you can destroy it.'

'You still would have killed me.'

'If I had hit you harder, and the Good Samaritan here hadn't rescued you, we wouldn't be having this conversation. Your death would have been a blessing, and it's not too late, is it?'

'Okay, it's a deal. When the police arrive, I'll make up an excuse, tell them that I was standing by the edge, feeding the ducks.'

'Rupert, make sure he keeps to his side of the bargain. And when the police are gone, come up to the house. I've something to show you.'

Margaret Wilmot left as quickly as she had come, leaving by the back door of the pub. She walked through the garden at the back and opened a gate onto the road on the far side. She then drove to her house. She was angry but elated. She had been a long time looking for that box, and it had taken that awful little bank manager to find it. She hoped the box contained what she wanted.

***

Tremayne didn't like the look of Cuthbert Wiggins. Not only was the man wrapped in a large blanket, but he sat perilously close to the heater. A wound could be seen on the left side of his head, the blood congealing in his matted hair.

'I'm fine, I'm telling you. If I hadn't been leaning over, I wouldn't have fallen and bashed my head on the way down.'

Clare phoned for an ambulance and a medic. Baxter, ordinarily sociable and ready to chat, was morose and holding back. Wiggins, who shouldn't have been in Compton, was coming up with feeble excuses.

'Where's your car?' Tremayne said.

'Up the road, where I fell in.'

'Why are you here, Wiggins? You're on bail, yet you keep putting yourself forward as something more. What's the truth, and don't give me any of that wanting to see where Gloria had spent the intervening years and how you two could have been something more. Gloria maltreated you, I'll grant you that, but you didn't come to the village on a nostalgia trip. You came here for a reason. It's the last will and testament of the woman. Did you find it? And the truth, not some half-hearted attempt at deflecting us. Quite frankly, Yarwood and I are tired of this village and its nefarious inhabitants. And you, Cuthbert Wiggins, are no better. You'd fit right in with this place.'

'I've nothing to say. I came here for no reason. Although I need to know if the cottage is mine. I've earned it, that's for sure.'

'For what? For not coming here before? What else do you know?'

While Tremayne kept up the heat on Wiggins, Clare went out through the front door of the pub and walked up to where his car was parked. She then phoned Jim Hughes, the crime scene examiner.

'Compton. There's been a development,' she said.

'Another body?'

'He should be, but he's still alive. We need you to check the man's car and where he fell in the river.'

At the pub, Tremayne kept probing. Too many years of policing had made him cautious. He did not like what he heard from Wiggins, nor Baxter's reticence.

'When did you arrive in Compton?' Tremayne asked.

'Last night.'

'And Baxter chose not to tell us, is that it?'

'I asked him to keep it secret. I met no one else, and he's the only one who knows I'm here.'

'Margaret knows,' Baxter said.

'How?'

'I told her this morning. She's been here, seen Wiggins, and left. Angry, as well.'

'Why the anger?'

'She told me I was a fool for not telling you about Wiggins.'

'At least someone's got a brain. Baxter, you're back as a major suspect, you realise that?'

'I've killed no one, and any attempts by you or anyone else to prove to the contrary will not succeed.'

Clare waited at Wiggins' car. Twenty-five minutes later, Jim Hughes arrived.

'It never ends, does it, with you and Tremayne?' Hughes said.

He kitted himself up, so did Clare; they moved over nearer to the car.

'Where he fell in is clear enough, but you said a bump on the head. It's just a muddy bank here, and there are no concealed rocks or branches that I can see.'

'That's why you're here. We're suspicious.'

Three more members of the crime scene investigation team arrived. A patrol car followed shortly afterwards. In the vehicle, the patrol officers and two uniforms.

Clare gathered the police around her. 'Tremayne's determined to crack this case today. We'll need you to be prepared, and if necessary, to bring anyone of interest to us. No doubt tempers will be frayed, but you know what to do.'

'Over here,' one of Hughes' team shouted.

Clare walked over to where the man was standing. 'What is it?'

'This branch, it's been used as a weapon.'

'A murder weapon?'

'Not if he's alive. We've also found footprints of another person. Wiggins' shoe size we know from the Underwood cottage, but this is larger, a riding boot, I'd say.'

'Female or male?'

'If it's a woman, she'd be a big woman, maybe taller than you.'

'Any way to prove conclusively?'

'Not here. We can try to match the shoe print to a manufacturer, and whoever wielded the branch was probably right-handed. Not sure if that helps much, but that's what we can see at this time. There doesn't appear to be much of interest in the car.'

'That's enough. Wiggins is claiming it was an accident, but if he had been hit on the head before falling in the water, then he's lying. The question is why.'

Chapter 26

Clare imagined that if the air had been calm and there was not the noise of vehicles in the distance, a low hum would have been heard in the air as the people in Compton indulged in what they enjoyed most – gossiping. In the vicinity of Wiggins' car, a group of people had gathered. Crime scene tape had been placed around the area, and those gawping, taking pictures with their smartphones and talking to each other and friends on the phone were not of primary interest to Clare. She spoke to two of them, and then passed on further questioning as well as obtaining names, addresses and phone numbers to the uniforms.

Opposite the pub, where Wiggins had pulled himself ashore, another two crime scene investigators were at work. Apart from the branch, and the prints of riding boots, no more evidence had been discovered.

Tremayne phoned. 'Get over to Margaret Wilmot. She's been in the pub, met Wiggins.'

Clare updated her senior with what had been found. 'It's not looking good for her,' she said.

'Wiggins is holding to his story, and Baxter's up to his neck in it.'

Clare drove through the village and took a right-hand turn up a winding road. At the end of it, the Wilmot manor house, the lady in question waiting at the door.

Clare looked down to notice that the woman was barefooted. 'Do you have a pair of riding boots?'

'Several. Why are you interested?'

'You were at the pub. You saw Cuthbert Wiggins.'

'I did.'

'Did you notice the wound on his head?'

'Damn silly thing to do, falling in the river like that. It's a wonder he's not dead.'

'That was the intention. Can I see your boots?' Clare insisted.

'If you must, but why? I go riding from time to time. I had a horse until a few years ago, but now I go to a riding stable not far from here. You can check if it's important.'

'Someone attempted to kill Mr Wiggins. Regardless of what he says, it wasn't an accident.'

'So why would he lie?'

'That's why I'm here. You seem to know everything that happens in this village.'

'I don't go around murdering people, and I certainly don't waste my time speculating, as apparently you do.'

'That's my job. But you do speculate, don't you? You speculate as to what would happen if you could separate the Woodcocks. What is it with Gwen? Something sinister, bedfellows, one of your ancestors planting their seed into Gwen's family? And why the

226

dislike of Barry? I'll grant you that he's not the smartest man, but he's honest and hardworking and a good family man.'

'You'd not understand. Gwen has been my friend for as long as I can remember. She could have made something of herself, and then she goes and gets pregnant to that man.'

'And what's wrong with him?'

'I told you once. I saw Barry Woodcock and James Baxter, and my husband was that way inclined, although not with Barry, too young for him.'

'There's a word for that, a phobia. Let's get back to Cuthbert Wiggins. Inspector Tremayne's with him now, and once he starts on someone that person will break eventually. I've got you down for the person who hit him, but why so close to home? You are meant to be a smart woman, so it must have been something important that he knew or maybe he had. Maybe it's the woman's missing will. If he's found it, then what interest is it to you?'

'I'm not a murderer.'

'You're the one with the riding gear. I don't think anyone else has the time or the money.'

'Gladys Upminster used to ride.'

'She's in prison.'

'You don't like me very much, do you?'

'My personal feelings are not important, only your guilt or innocence.'

'Come into the house,' Margaret said. 'I've got something to show you.'

Clare entered, noticing a crack in the wall in the main hall that hadn't been there on her previous visit. To the right of the main entrance, a large wooden door.

Margaret Wilmot pushed it open and beckoned for Clare to follow.

Inside, a bibliophile's heaven. There were books stacked in shelving up to the ceiling. Clare estimated the height of the room to be at least sixteen to seventeen feet. 'There must be close to forty thousand books in here,' she said.

'It's nearer to sixty thousand. The Wilmots were always great believers in education and the arts.'

'And you?'

'I do what I can, but times have changed. The wealth disparity of the past no longer exists, and libraries such as this cost a fortune to maintain.'

'You sound as though you regret the demise of feudalism.'

'It is what allowed places such as this library, this house, to exist, and now Barry Woodcock is the future. Gwen used to love coming in here and reading. I saw a possibility in her, a chance to rise above the crowd, to become a woman of substance.'

'That was her choice,' Clare said. 'She chose Barry, and from what I can see, she's happy.'

'Happiness is not the right of a person. It is more important to achieve, to strive, to better one's self.'

'We're digressing,' Clare said. 'The fact remains that you are the only person in this village who is a possibility for the attempted murder of Cuthbert Wiggins. Will you allow a search of your house?'

'I've nothing to hide.'

'That wasn't the question. Will you allow a search of your house?'

'I will not. This is a gross insult.'

'Very well. I phoned on the way up here to a colleague at Bemerton Road Police Station. A request for a search warrant is with the magistrate now, and I expect it to be granted within the next few hours. You can either come up to the pub or I'll stay here while we wait.'

'My Member of Parliament will hear of this. He's a personal friend.'

Clare remembered what Tremayne always said when they mentioned their influential friends: guilty.

***

'Now look here, Wiggins,' Tremayne said, revived after a cigarette outside the pub and a hot drink supplied by Baxter. 'You're in the village for a reason, and that's three times we know of in total. What's the real reason this time? You couldn't go and see Stephanie Underwood as she's dead. You couldn't come and visit Gloria's grave because she isn't buried yet. Whatever it is, it's serious, and neither you nor I, not anyone else in this village, is going anywhere until you tell me the truth.'

'My wife's worried. I should phone her,' Wiggins said.

'You have already. Phone her if you want, but there's no more to say other than you'll have a comfy cell tonight unless I get some answers.'

'The bank's not waiting until the trial. As far as they are concerned, I'm guilty.'

'There must be a severance package.'

'Enough to live on, and my wife is not demanding. We'll survive, but I'm still young. I can't retire, not now, and no one else in the banking industry will give me a job, even if I'm vindicated.'

'Life's not fair, you must have heard that adage.'

'I'm entitled to be treated with more respect. After all that I did for the bank.'

'Play your violin if you want, but if you're after sympathy, you'll not get it from me. You're here in Compton for a reason, not just a sightseeing trip, and if it's not legal, you're in trouble. And we have proof that you didn't fall into the water, someone hit you with a branch. It's attempted murder, but you're here protecting whoever, and the only two we know of are Margaret Wilmot and Rupert Baxter, and I wouldn't trust either.'

'I don't know what you mean. I slipped, that's all.'

'I told you once before,' Tremayne said, 'you're a lousy liar. Not only are you sitting there trying to pretend that nothing's wrong, but you're still shivering, the wound on your head looks as though it could do with some more treatment, and you're averting your eyes. Each time you lie, you look away. I've counted five times now, and in my book, you're guilty of a crime, but I'm not sure which one. Maybe you killed Gloria.'

'I didn't. I swear it.'

'Wiggins, your continual denials are not helping you at all. It could be that you visited Gloria in her cottage, tried to talk some sense into her and asked her for money. Your wife must hate living next door to those neighbours of yours, and Gloria is down here with your money. Maybe you thought that you could appeal to her better nature, assumed that she had mellowed with time.'

'You've got it all wrong. The woman would never mellow, I knew that. She was as cold as ice back then, and she still is.'

'Is? The woman's dead. Level with me, when did you last see Gloria Wiggins?'

'That day she took my money. I've told you this before.'

Tremayne was confused. In front of him was a man who had nearly died at the hands of another, yet he continued to deny the fact, or to admit to any wrongdoing. He left him in the company of a uniform and went back to Rupert Baxter, who Tremayne could see was up to his neck in it.

'That's the truth,' Baxter said. He pushed a pint of beer over the counter to Tremayne, who declined. He did not intend to be deflected by an act of generosity from a man who was a crucial witness and a probable murderer.

'What truth? You go and rescue Wiggins from the other side of the river. The man's been in the water. He's got a gash on the back of his head, and you just pick him up and bring him to the pub. Weren't you curious?'

'Of course, but the man's condition was more important, and I did phone you as soon as I could.'

'What's Margaret Wilmot's involvement in all this? We're going to check her house, and if we find proof that she tried to kill Wiggins, then you're an accomplice.'

'I've killed no one, and I'll not allow you or anyone else, not even Margaret, to implicate me.'

'But you know who killed the others, don't you?'

Baxter stood back from Tremayne. He said nothing.

'Come on, Baxter, out with it. What do you know?'

'I've been giving some thought to it.'

'Baxter, you're a man who doesn't miss much, and this story that Wiggins is giving me is just nonsense. Either you or Margaret hit him, and as to why he's protecting you both, I don't know. But I intend to find out, and if I don't, I'll have you and your girlfriend down at Bemerton Road, and it won't be as cosy as here.'

231

'Inspector, you're threatening me. I could make a complaint of harassment. There must be a complaints department at your police station.'

'I'll give you their phone number if you want, but first, what is it with Wiggins? The man must know that someone tried to kill him, but he's keeping quiet. You're a smart man, by your own admission, and Margaret Wilmot's nobody's fool. This romance of yours, it is above board, or is it all a subterfuge?'

'What do you mean?'

'What I said. You're not a matched pair, and maybe nothing is going on, just you two getting together to hatch a plan.'

'There's nothing. Margaret's a tough woman, but she'll use the legal process to achieve her aims, and I'm not a criminal. You can check, you'll find nothing against me.'

***

Clare was equally frustrated at the manor house. Not only would Margaret Wilmot not let her into the house, but she was also determined to evict Clare from her premises, the grounds included. If she weren't nearby, Clare knew that the woman would have a chance to destroy the evidence and to come up with an excuse. Outside, on the road, Clare could see the Woodcocks, the old Land Rover now fixed as it had transported Barry and Gwen to the scene.

Clare phoned for back up, the patrol car that was in the village driving the short distance up to the house. Another patrol car was on its way from Salisbury, as were two more uniforms. The scene was being set for a showdown, Clare thought, as in an old cowboy movie, where the forces of right were lined up against the forces of wrong. Clare was not sure who was the wrong at the present time, but instinct, the sixth sense that a police officer hopes to gain with time and experience, was kicking in.

'You're hindering a murder investigation,' Clare said to Margaret Wilmot. 'A search warrant is on its way, and if we find anything, it'll go against you.'

'I've nothing to hide. I resent being treated in this manner.'

'We'll be checking the other houses in the village, not only yours. And our crime scene investigators have a clearer idea of who hit Cuthbert Wiggins. What's the truth? What did you say down at the pub to make the man go silent? What's this great secret that you're hiding?'

Chapter 27

Tremayne continued to wrestle with the recalcitrant survivor of a murder attempt and a smart man masquerading as a jovial publican; neither man excited the straightforward and honest police inspector. Tremayne was sure that Margaret Wilmot, Rupert Baxter, and now Cuthbert Wiggins were in league with each other. Not one of them could be trusted, not by Tremayne and Clare, nor by each other. And what was it that Wiggins wanted? According to him, it was the last will and testament, but with the man being so difficult, Tremayne wasn't so sure that Gloria, painted as the villain, hadn't been maligned.

'Baxter, Sergeant Yarwood's up at the Wilmot house. She's not leaving until she's had the place searched, and now the Woodcocks are sniffing around. If somebody doesn't start giving some honest answers to my questions, then I'll arrest the whole damn irritating lot of you and throw you all in the cells at the police station.'

'You'll be open to accusations of wrongful arrest.'

'What happens to me doesn't matter. My career's in rundown mode, and if I don't solve these murders, it'll be the end for me. And I don't care how smart you are, you're guilty of one crime, probably more. And you and Wiggins are in collusion, as is Margaret Wilmot.'

'Tremayne, you're a bastard, you know that?'

'I do, but when I see people lying through their teeth, I get angry, and when I'm angry, I become unpredictable.'

'We've done nothing wrong,' Baxter said. 'Wiggins shouldn't have been in the village, and someone had it in for him.'

'Who? The man was meant to be an enigma, a fiction of Gloria Wiggins' imagination. Are you saying that some people knew that he wasn't, and the man had a secret so important that his death was warranted?'

'I don't know the full story. In fact, I don't know any of it. Gloria and this working in a bank, we didn't know about. For whatever reason, she always made it out to be something more.'

'What if it was?' Tremayne said.

'Wiggins would know.'

'And he's in the next room. Why was he parked just up the road?'

Wiggins came out from the other room. 'I heard you speaking about me,' he said.

'Tremayne is certain that you and Gloria did more than work in a bank,' Baxter said. The police inspector knew that what he had said to Baxter regarding disciplinaries and wrongful arrests wasn't altogether truthful. He didn't want his career to end with a black mark, the ignominy of a police officer who had stayed for one more murder investigation than he should have and had failed to solve it.

'It was a bank, nothing more. Gloria was a bank teller back then, and I was heading into management. For some reason, she wasn't interested in a career, and now we know why, don't we?'

'Do we?' Tremayne said.

'I was the bank, not that I was worth a fortune, but it was enough for her. I don't know how she succeeded in this village without cheating others.'

'Maybe she did,' Tremayne said. 'Baxter, you'd better level with me. Yarwood's got the warrant now, and I've got Margaret Wilmot down for the person who hit Wiggins over the head. It's either you for murder or her.'

'Wiggins didn't die.'

'A technicality. And what about the others? You've got the build to handle a chainsaw, but that would have taken someone sick in the head to carve up Sheila Blatchford. Are you that person? Genius-level intellect coupled with a sadistic madness. Is that why you chose to hide yourself down here in Compton? Is there something up in Oxford? Unsolved murders, bodies in shallow graves?'

'You've got it all wrong,' Baxter said. Tremayne noticed that the man was standing back, not so sure of himself.

***

Eustace Upminster arrived in Compton. He was in the company of Linda Wilson who was driving her Audi. One of the uniforms who had been at the Upminsters on the day he had been knifed recognised him. The uniform phoned Clare who called Tremayne.

Twenty minutes after they had entered the village, the two of them were in the pub. Tremayne had realised that he was getting nowhere fast with Wiggins and Baxter. He needed to give them time to dwell on the parlous situation both of them were in.

'Upminster, what brings you to Compton, and why have you come with Linda Wilson?' Tremayne said.

'I needed to visit the farm. I've been to see Gladys and to forgive her.'

'Yet you're here with another woman.'

'I'm a friend, and Eustace can't drive,' Linda Wilson said.

'Don't try to make something out of it,' Upminster said. 'Linda's been honest with you when you questioned her before. There are no skeletons to rattle, and Gladys knew about Linda and me.'

'It's still a motive for attempted murder, and what about the others? What do you have to say? I've got Baxter pretending to be a saint, and Cuthbert Wiggins lying through his teeth. What's the truth? Why are you here in Compton? You can barely walk, and Miss Wilson's hanging on to you to stop you falling over. It seems more than a friendship to me.'

'Linda, how are you?' Baxter said.

'Rupert, I'm fine. A long time,' the woman replied.

'Another of your customers?' Tremayne said. Her status in the village, before regarded as benign and a minor player, had changed. She was a woman who had been in the underbelly of life; a woman who would know how to be devious and to exude charm and beauty while committing murder.

'I last saw Rupert when we were a lot younger and a lot thinner. Inspector Tremayne, I'm not a common prostitute. I do not conduct business in my own backyard, and Rupert couldn't afford me.'

'Inspector, you're clutching at straws,' Baxter said. 'Nobody's guilty here, and we'd appreciate it if you'd go somewhere else. I've got a business to run, and you're not helping.'

'This pub stays closed until further notice. And if you don't like it, you can complain to Superintendent Moulton. This case is going to be solved today, and you, Rupert Baxter, are going to start talking.'

***

Clare moved through the manor house. She was accompanied by two uniforms. Margaret Wilmot had objected, even after being presented with the search warrant duly signed. Her objection had been noted, and she was now in the back of a police car. She was not restrained, but it had been made clear that any further disruption by her would be regarded as suspicious.

Inside the house, Clare moved from the front to the back, the two uniforms taking the rooms to either side of the long hallway. Apart from a smell of damp and decay, there was nothing noteworthy. The building was old, and there were nooks and crannies in abundance, even loose wall panels, and cupboards that wouldn't open. Clare could see a long day ahead, although the time from the attempted murder of Cuthbert Wiggins to the time that she and Tremayne had arrived in the village hadn't been long. Clare hoped the woman's arrogance, her ultimate belief in her superiority, would be enough to have made her careless.

A small team of crime scene investigators were also in the house, initially conducting an exercise to see if there were any signs linking the house and the woman to any of the murders. If they or Clare and the uniforms found anything of interest, then there would be a full mobilisation and the house would be subjected to a rigorous investigation. In the kitchen, the oven was hot; inside a cake was baking. To one side of the oven, a pantry. Clare opened it to find a pair of boots on the floor; they were still muddy.

'I need you up at the manor house,' Clare said on the phone to Jim Hughes. 'Your team will need to go through this house with a fine-tooth comb.'

***

Hamish and Desdemona Foster appeared at the pub twenty-five minutes after they were summoned by Tremayne, as did the Woodcocks. Clare arrived after thirty.

Margaret Wilmot, now aware of what had been found in the pantry, reacted calmly to the news that the crime scene investigators would be comparing the boots found to the boot prints at the river. Also, she had been informed that she would need to supply a DNA sample, as a broken nail had been found lodged under the bark of the branch, the intended murder weapon. Another court order was being obtained to make her comply, and whereas she was still a free woman, her movements were being monitored, a uniform assigned to her.

In the end, the woman had come to the pub in Clare's car. She had said little on the way, and Clare could see that her typical arrogance had been replaced by something more contrite.

Inside the pub, a murderer sat. Tremayne had his suspicions, as had Clare. Cuthbert Wiggins sat quietly to one side. The others looked at him, some had asked his name. Most had been surprised to finally meet Gloria Wiggins' phantom husband.

'Never expected to see you here,' Hamish Foster said.

'I didn't like her,' Barry Woodcock said. 'And you were married to her?'

'I was,' the only reply from Wiggins.

Outside the pub were two patrol cars, another two uniforms, and some of the crime scene investigators.

'I intended to conduct this investigation differently today, individual interviews,' Tremayne said. He was standing up and addressing those assembled. 'However, you have precipitated a different approach.'

'How?' Baxter asked.

'We never expected Eustace Upminster to be in Compton, nor Linda Wilson. And as for Cuthbert Wiggins, his arrival in the village came as a complete surprise. We expect to charge one person here with murder within the next hour.'

'Who?' Hamish Foster said.

'Let us go through the case so far,' Tremayne said, purposely ignoring the question, wanting them to sweat some more.

'I resent my being here,' Margaret Wilmot said.

'Duly noted,' Clare said. 'However, Inspector Tremayne is within his rights to conduct this interview. Miss Wilmot, in your case, I would suggest that you do not interrupt anymore. We believe that you are guilty of the attempted murder of Cuthbert Wiggins, and we will be charging you subject to a phone call from the crime scene investigators up at your house.'

'Let me come back to where I was,' Tremayne said. 'Gloria Wiggins was killed for a reason. The assumption was that she was a difficult woman who had

240

alienated certain people in this village. And we all know about James Baxter and his relationship with Barry Woodcock, and what the woman said about James and his subsequent death. That was an accident caused by Gloria Wiggins' venomous tongue.'

'You've no right to speak ill of the dead,' Desdemona Foster said. 'It's disrespectful.'

'It's a murder investigation, not a memorial service for the dear departed. I'll say whatever needs to be said. Gloria Wiggins was not a good person, and her former husband, Cuthbert Wiggins, will back this up.'

'I will,' Wiggins said.

'After Gloria Wiggins died, then we had Bert Blatchford and his wife. Whoever killed Sheila Blatchford must have a sadistic nature, the sort of person who pulled the wings off butterflies as a child. Does anyone want to proffer a name as to who it may be?'

No one spoke.

'Very well, but remember that whoever dissected that woman with a chainsaw is in this room, and they could do the same to any of you here. Not today or tomorrow, but anytime in the future, and this time he may not even garrotte you before slicing you with the weapon.'

'Please, no more,' Desdemona Foster said.

'Mrs Foster, you're right. It's not a pleasant subject, but then, murder isn't,' Tremayne said. 'You couldn't have killed Sheila, as it would have required someone with more strength, but you may know who it is. Your husband, for instance?'

'I've killed no one,' Hamish Foster said. 'What about Eustace Upminster? Barry Woodcock? It was Woodcock's chainsaw, wasn't it?'

'It was, but he didn't kill Sheila, Gwen did.'

Clare looked over at Tremayne, wondered where he had got that notion from, before realising that he was throwing a cat amongst the pigeons. The man was looking for a reaction, for tempers to flare, and to create confusion and uncertainty amongst those assembled.

Barry Woodcock was on his feet, his arm around his wife who was in tears. 'How dare you,' she said.

'You bastard. My wife did not kill Sheila Blatchford, and you said before that she wouldn't have been strong enough, whereas I was,' Barry Woodcock said.

'Did I, or was I just saying it for a reaction, the same as I am now. And yes, your wife did not kill Sheila, but we know who attempted to kill Cuthbert Wiggins.'

'I fell in the water,' Wiggins said.

Clare went over to the Woodcocks and asked them to sit down; they complied.

'Lies,' Tremayne said. 'We have the CSIs over at Gloria's cottage. You've been in there, no doubt looking for her last will and testament. Did you find it?'

'Okay, I was there. I'll admit to it, but no. I don't have it yet.'

'But you know where it is?'

'No.'

'Why under the bed? How did you know about her hiding it there? You can at least answer that.'

'Gloria always kept her important documents close to her. I remembered that the other day. I only wanted the document, and I didn't kill anyone.'

'How did you get into the cottage?'

'A key buried next to one of the trees outside. That's what she did when we lived together. I assumed that was what she would have done in Compton. I took a chance and found it within five minutes. After that, I was only interested in the will.'

'It was in a cavity under the floor. It's not going to be lying there with the insects and the dust.'

'It was wrapped in plastic.'

'They'll eat through that. It must have been in something solid, a box of some sort.'

'There is a metal box near where we found the boots,' Clare said. 'It's old and rusty.'

'That's my property. It's nothing to do with this investigation,' Margaret Wilmot said.

'Yarwood, get the CSIs to check it out quickly and get it over here,' Tremayne said.

'I'm already on to it.'

'If it's the box, then why is it at your house? What else is in that box? Blackmail, is that it? But you were friendly with the woman.'

'I was never friendly. We shared a common belief in what was good for the village, and I had seen Rupert's brother and Barry Woodcock.'

'And now Rupert's your lover. We've never understood you and him. You two have nothing perceivable in common. You're an embittered woman, he's an academic who prefers village life, the lure of a fish and a pint of beer.'

'Our relationship is not your concern,' Baxter said.

'It is when Margaret attempts to kill Wiggins, and the three of you cook up a story to cover what's happened. And why? It's what's in that box, and now we have it, and you three are going to be charged either with attempted murder or perverting the course of justice. What is it, Wiggins? So far, you will avoid a prison term and will more than likely be held over for community service. Do you want to go to prison for concealing an attempted murder? You've nothing to gain now from holding out on the truth.'

'I only want what is rightfully mine, and my wife deserves a better life.'

'The box at Margaret Wilmot's, is it Gloria's box?'

'If it's rusty and red, then yes. I only went along with the two of them as Margaret Wilmot said that she'd let me have what was mine once she had opened it.'

'He's lying,' Margaret Wilmot said.

'The box is on its way over now,' Clare said. 'One of the CSIs has opened it.'

'My property, is it in there?' Wiggins asked.

'We don't know yet. And what will be found of yours, Margaret Wilmot?'

'I've nothing to say. This is pure conjecture, and I will not say another word without my lawyer present.'

'Very well. The CSIs are confirming that your boots were down at the river with Wiggins. They'll be passing them on to Forensics for further examination. Also, a court order will force you to give a sample of your DNA. We have enough to charge you with attempted murder.'

'Ask one of the uniforms to come in,' Tremayne said to Clare. 'We'll charge Margaret Wilmot in the other room and inform her of her rights.'

'I'm innocent.'

'No, you're not,' Wiggins said. 'I only went along because you said that you'd give me what I wanted out of that box, and I'll testify that it was the same box that Gloria had all those years ago when we were married, and that you, Margaret Wilmot, admitted to my attempted murder. And Baxter was present.'

'Mr Baxter, you're an accomplice after the fact to the attempted murder of Cuthbert Wiggins. You will also be charged,' Tremayne said.

***

After forty minutes, Clare and Tremayne returned to where the others were sitting. Margaret Wilmot, now charged with murder, sat separately from the others, as did Rupert Baxter. Margaret was handcuffed, Baxter was not.

'That's two of the major crimes solved,' Tremayne said. 'We have a murderer for Stephanie Underwood, but not for the others. Gloria Wiggins was unconscious when she was strung up, and the contents of the box will reveal why Cuthbert was attacked. However, Gloria's death is unrelated. You, Margaret Wilmot, wanted the woman alive, at least until the box had been found. Wiggins coming to this village was fortunate for you, in that he was the only person who knew where the box was. His finding it condemned him. The box is here with us now. Do you want to tell us what is in it?'

'I've no more to say. I need my lawyer to be here.'

'You are no longer needed. There is a patrol car outside, and you will be transferred to Bemerton Road Police Station. We will talk again, either today or tomorrow. You did not kill any of the others. Baxter will stay here as he is still involved.'

One of the uniforms took hold of Margaret Wilmot and led her out of the pub. Inside, the others sat silent.

'We still have two murders to solve,' Tremayne said.

'Don't you mean three?' Eustace Upminster said.

245

'We know who killed Gloria. It's only the Blatchfords who concern us now.'

'I didn't kill her,' Wiggins said.

'You did not. We did not find her last will and testament. However, we did find a photo of your wife.'

'I don't understand.'

'You do. Gloria Wiggins and your wife knew each other. And judging by the photo, they were friends. It looks to be after you and Gloria divorced. What did your wife know and for how long?'

'She knew how Gloria treated me, and yes, they were friends once. I didn't know that when I met my wife. Gloria didn't come straight back to the village after taking my money, and for another six to nine months she worked in another bank, but you know this.'

'We do, but we didn't know about the friendship. You told us that your wife had seen Gloria's cottage briefly once, but never Gloria. Why did you lie?'

'It didn't seem important, and if you knew, you'd suspect my wife. I'd do anything to protect her.'

'Even murder?'

'Even that.'

'Your wife knew about Gloria burying a spare key in the garden. The key has been retrieved and is on its way to Forensics. The CSIs have checked it out first. There are fingerprints on the bag it was in, not many and they're difficult to identify, but they believe they've found your wife's. She had been at the house, she killed Gloria.'

'No, never. Not my wife.'

'Your wife is house-proud, and she's a loyal wife living in a bad neighbourhood. You may have planted the seed in her mind that if your former wife died earlier rather than later, then your lives would be better.'

'She would never kill anyone.'

'Unfortunately, she's been confronted with the truth, and she has admitted to her crime. Why we didn't pick up on this before is unclear. Apart from the key, we found no other evidence of her being at Gloria's cottage.'

'I want to be with her,' Wiggins said.

'After further questioning at Bemerton Road Police Station, but not today. Your wife will be formally charged at the police station nearest to your house. Tomorrow morning, she will be transferred to Salisbury. You can see her then.'

'Gloria was a big woman; my wife is smaller than her.'

'An angry and desperate woman can summon an unknown strength. If your wife was desperate enough and hated the woman as much as you did, then it's possible. How Stephanie Underwood failed to hear what was happening next door, we can't be sure. She may have been involved, but that seems unlikely.'

'That still leaves the murders of Bert and Sheila Blatchford,' Clare said.

'Are you saying one of us sitting here is guilty?' Hamish Foster asked. He had his arm around Desdemona, almost concealing her from view.

'There was more than one photo in the box. In fact, over the years the woman had compiled a photographic dossier of those of interest. Eustace, there's a photo of you with Linda, but it's not recent. We'll check, but it goes back about ten years, and it was at your farm. Was your wife away at that time?'

'It's not a reason for murder.'

'It's not. And Linda Wilson is innocent of the crime of murder, although if bad judgement were a crime, then she'd be guilty. For whatever reason, she's fond of you, and I'm not sure that you deserve it.'

'I loved Eustace. If he hadn't been so loyal to Gladys, then we'd be together.'

'Let's backtrack,' Tremayne said. 'We know that in their youth, Baxter, Eustace Upminster, and Hamish Foster used to go out and about and that Stephanie Underwood and Gloria Wiggins, possibly Margaret Wilmot, were receptive to their inherent charms. Barry Woodcock was not involved, as he wasn't interested in women, only Gwen, but he's not a man with a strong sex drive. Is that correct?'

'How dare you insult my husband,' Gwen Woodcock said.

'I deal in facts, not insults,' Tremayne said. 'The photos in the box confirm some of the relationships, even Barry and James Baxter. A distant shot and not focussed, but it's clear who it is and what they are doing. We're assuming that Gloria took the shot, although it may have been Margaret. Besides, it's not important at this time. What is more important is that Gloria had a copy of a document disputing the Wilmots' claim on some of the land in this village, in particular the Woodcocks' farm. How she obtained this document and when are unknown, but Margaret Wilmot would clearly have wanted it.'

'So would we,' Gwen Woodcock said.

'Margaret did not kill Gloria or the Blatchfords, although Gloria, judging by her bank statements, received small amounts into her account from unknown persons. We suspect that she may have been using her knowledge of this village and its inhabitants to coerce payments.'

'Blackmail?'

'She would have said it was gifts, and no one would have complained to the police. As I said, small amounts, and not sufficient to cause anyone financial hardship, but over the years the money has added up. She

248

knew about Barry and James. She knew about Eustace and Linda. Did she ever contact you, Miss Wilson?'

'No.'

'She contacted me,' Upminster said. 'Nothing serious, more of an insinuation.'

'You gave her money?'

'Some, but it was more of a donation. She said she was struggling to pay a bill, and would I help. Nothing more than that.'

'You're protecting a devious woman. Why?'

'There's no more to say.'

Tremayne could see everyone going around in a circle, being obtuse as usual. He needed to raise the ire of those in the room. He looked over at Clare. She knew what to do.

'Desdemona, why did you kill Bert Blatchford?' Clare said.

'How dare you accuse my wife,' Hamish Foster said.

'We have a photo of Desdemona holding Bert Blatchford's hand. They are both young, in their teens.'

'I thought the contents of the box were about Margaret,' Desdemona said quietly.

'We've addressed that. Were you romantically involved with Bert Blatchford?'

'My father was a tyrant. He would have beaten me if he had known, but yes.'

'Does your husband know?'

'Yes, but it was a long time ago, before I married Hamish.'

'So why did you kill him?'

'He was going to tell everyone. He wanted money, a lot of it, more than we could spare. I couldn't deal with the shame.'

Tremayne realised that, as so often happens, the need to confess comes at the most unexpected moment.

'We've always had you as a weak and timid woman.'

'I am, but Hamish doesn't deserve to be embarrassed by my past.'

'It's not a reason to kill someone.'

'If you had known my father and what he beat into me, it was. I saw Bert there with his pigs, and I tried to reason with him, but he wouldn't budge. Either I paid, or he said that he'd make me out to be the local tart. I couldn't allow that.'

'The knife?'

'I had it in my hand. I was going to threaten him with it. It was an accident, I swear it, but he turned his back on me, called me some offensive words, and then the knife was there in his back, and he was on the ground with the pigs.'

'We found no proof that you had been there.'

'I was careful to conceal the evidence, and I took my time to check. Sheila wasn't there, so it was Bert and me.'

'And how did you feel afterwards?'

'I felt nothing, only relief.'

'My wife doesn't realise what she's saying,' Hamish Foster said.

'It doesn't matter now,' Desdemona said. 'The truth is important.'

'Hamish Foster, you killed Sheila Blatchford,' Tremayne said.

'I tried to reason with Sheila who had figured out that it was Desdemona. She was as heartless as Gloria. Sheila wanted money, more than Bert, for her silence. I couldn't let it continue.'

250

Another confession, as unexpected as the first one. Both Tremayne and Clare were pleased that their time in Compton had concluded; sorry that yet again decent people had committed terrible crimes for which they would have to pay.

'The chainsaw?'

'I knew where Woodcock kept it, and I knew how to get into his barn. Two days after I had confronted Sheila, I found her in the barn. I strangled her, but anger at what I'd done, and then revulsion, made me decide to hide the evidence.'

'Why take a chainsaw if you hadn't intended to use it?'

'I had, and then I changed my mind, but when I saw her looking at me with her eyes wide open as I killed her, I knew I had to complete what I had originally set out to do. I changed my clothes and placed them outside the back of the barn. I then went back and did what I had to.'

'We never understood how you cleaned yourself up afterwards.'

'There's a small stream not far away. I washed there and put on the clothes that I had left outside of the barn. It rained heavily that night, so I suppose any sign of my walking across to the stream was washed away.'

'Weren't you revolted by what you had done?'

'I had saved Desdemona from embarrassment. I felt numb, but nothing more.'

Tremayne stood outside the pub. The Fosters had been charged and were on their way to the cells at the police station. Eustace Upminster was getting cosy with Linda Wilson. The Woodcocks were back with their children at their farm.

'Superintendent Moulton will be after your retirement now,' Clare said as Tremayne lit up a cigarette.

'Death holds no fear, retirement does,' Tremayne said as he took his first puff.

The End

ALSO BY THE AUTHOR

Death by a Dead Man's Hand – A DI Tremayne Thriller

A flawed heist of forty gold bars from a security van late at night. One of the perpetrators is killed by his brother as they argue over what they have stolen.

Eighteen years later, the murderer, released after serving his sentence for his brother's murder, waits in a church for a man purporting to be the brother he killed. And then he too is killed.

The threads stretch back a long way, and now more people are dying in the search for the missing gold bars.

Detective Inspector Tremayne, his health causing him concern, and Sergeant Clare Yarwood, still seeking romance, are pushed to the limit solving the murder, attempting to prevent any more.

Death at Coombe Farm – A DI Tremayne Thriller

A warring family. A disputed inheritance. A recipe for death.

If it hadn't been for the circumstances, Detective Inspector Keith Tremayne would have said the view was outstanding. Up high, overlooking the farmhouse in the valley below, the panoramic vista of Salisbury Plain stretching out beyond. The only problem was that near where he stood with his sergeant, Clare Yarwood, there was a body, and it wasn't a pleasant sight.

Death and the Lucky Man – A DI Tremayne Thriller

Sixty-eight million pounds and dead. Hardly the outcome expected for the luckiest man in England the day his lottery ticket was drawn out of the barrel. But then, Alan Winters' rags-to-riches story had never been conventional, and there were those who had benefited, but others who hadn't.

Death and the Assassin's Blade – A DI Tremayne Thriller

It was meant to be high drama, not murder, but someone's switched the daggers. The man's death took place in plain view of two serving police officers.

He was not meant to die; the daggers were only theatrical props, plastic and harmless. A summer's night, a production of Julius Caesar amongst the ruins of an Anglo-Saxon fort. Detective Inspector Tremayne is there with his sergeant, Clare Yarwood. In the assassination scene, Caesar collapses to the ground. Brutus defends his actions; Mark Antony rebukes him.

They're a disparate group, the amateur actors. One's an estate agent, another an accountant. And then there is the teenage school student, the gay man, the funeral director. And what about the women? They could be involved.

They've each got a secret, but which of those on the stage wanted Gordon Mason, the actor who had portrayed Caesar, dead?

Death Unholy – A DI Tremayne Thriller

All that remained were the man's two legs and a chair full of greasy and fetid ash. Little did DI Keith Tremayne know that it was the beginning of a journey into the murky world of paganism and its ancient rituals. And it was going to get very dangerous.

'Do you believe in spontaneous human combustion?' Detective Inspector Keith Tremayne asked.

'Not me. I've read about it. Who hasn't?' Sergeant Clare Yarwood answered.

'I haven't,' Tremayne replied, which did not surprise his young sergeant. In the months they had been working together, she had come to realise that he was a man who had little interest in the world. When he had a cigarette in his mouth, a beer in his hand, and a murder to solve he was about the happiest she ever saw him, but even then he could hardly be regarded as one of life's most sociable people. And as for reading? The most he managed was an occasional police report, an early morning newspaper, turning first to the back pages for the racing results.

Murder of a Silent Man – A DCI Cook Thriller

A murdered recluse. A property empire. A disinherited family – All the ingredients for murder.

No one gave much credence to the man when he was alive. In fact, most people never knew who he was, although those who had lived in the area for many years recognised the tired-looking and shabbily-dressed man as he shuffled along, regular as clockwork on a Thursday afternoon at seven in the evening to the local off-licence. It was always the same: a bottle of whisky, premium brand, and a packet of cigarettes. He paid his money over the counter, took hold of his plastic bag containing his purchases, and then walked back down the road with the same rhythmic shuffle. He said not one word to anyone on the street or in the shop.

Murder in Room 346 – A DCI Cook Thriller

'Coitus interruptus, that's what it is,' Detective Chief Inspector Isaac Cook said. On the bed, in a downmarket hotel in Bayswater, lay the naked bodies of a man and a woman.

'Bullet in the head's not the way to go,' Larry Hill, Isaac Cook's detective inspector, said. He had not expected such a flippant comment from his senior, not when they were standing near to two people who had, apparently in the final throes of passion, succumbed to what appeared to be a professional assassination.

'You know this will be all over the media within the hour,' Isaac said.

'James Holden, moral crusader, a proponent of the sanctity of the marital bed, man and wife. It's bound to be.'

Murder in Notting Hill – A DCI Cook Thriller

One murderer, two bodies, two locations, and the murders have been committed within an hour of each other.

They're separated by a couple of miles, and neither woman has anything in common with the other. One is young and wealthy, the daughter of a famous man; the other is poor, hardworking and unknown.

Isaac Cook and his team at Challis Street Police Station are baffled about why they've been killed. There must be a connection, but what is it?

Murder is the Only Option – A DCI Cook Thriller

A man, thought to be long dead, returns to exact revenge against those who had blighted his life. His only concern is to protect his wife and daughter. He will stop at nothing to achieve his aim.

'Big Greg, I never expected to see you around here at this time of night.'

'I've told you enough times.'

'I've no idea what you're talking about,' Robertson replied. He looked up at the man, only to see a metal pole coming down at him. Robertson fell down, cracking his head against a concrete kerb.

Two vagrants, no more than twenty feet away, did not stir and did not even look in the direction of the noise. If they had, they would have seen a dead body, another man walking away.

Murder in Little Venice – A DCI Cook Thriller

A dismembered corpse floats in the canal in Little Venice, an upmarket tourist haven in London. Its identity is unknown, but what is its significance?

DCI Isaac Cook is baffled about why it's there. Is it gang-related, or is it something more?

Whatever the reason, it's clearly a warning, and Isaac and his team are sure it's not the last body that they'll have to deal with.

Murder is Only a Number – A DCI Cook Thriller

Before she left she carved a number in blood on his chest. But why the number 2, if this was her first murder?

The woman prowls the streets of London. Her targets are men who have wronged her. Or have they? And why is she keeping count?

DCI Cook and his team finally know who she is, but not before she's murdered four men. The whole team are looking for her, but the woman keeps disappearing in plain sight. The pressure's on to stop her, but she's always one step ahead.

And this time, DCS Goddard can't protect his protégé, Isaac Cook, from the wrath of the new commissioner at the Met.

Murder House – A DCI Cook Thriller

A corpse in the fireplace of an old house. It's been there for thirty years, but who is it?

It's murder, but who is the victim and what connection does the body have to the previous owners of the house. What is the motive? And why is the body in a fireplace? It was bound to be discovered eventually but was that what the murderer wanted? The main suspects are all old and dying, or already dead.

Isaac Cook and his team have their work cut out trying to put the pieces together. Those who know are not talking because of an old-fashioned belief that a family's dirty laundry should not be aired in public, and never to a policeman – even if that means the murderer is never brought to justice!

Murder is a Tricky Business – A DCI Cook Thriller

A television actress is missing, and DCI Isaac Cook, the Senior Investigation Officer of the Murder Investigation Team at Challis Street Police Station in London, is searching for her.

Why has he been taken away from more important crimes to search for the woman? It's not the first time she's gone missing, so why does everyone assume she's been murdered?

There's a secret, that much is certain, but who knows it? The missing woman? The executive producer? His eavesdropping assistant? Or the actor who portrayed her fictional brother in the TV soap opera?

Murder Without Reason – A DCI Cook Thriller

DCI Cook faces his greatest challenge. The Islamic State is waging war in England, and they are winning.

Not only does Isaac Cook have to contend with finding the perpetrators, but he is also being forced to commit actions contrary to his mandate as a police officer.

And then there is Anne Argento, the prime minister's deputy. The prime minister has shown himself to be a pacifist and is not up to the task. She needs to take his job if the country is to fight back against the Islamists.

Vane and Martin have provided the solution. Will DCI Cook and Anne Argento be willing to follow it through? Are they able to act for the good of England, knowing that a criminal and murderous action is about to take place? Do they have an option?

The Haberman Virus

A remote and isolated village in the Hindu Kush
mountain range in North Eastern Afghanistan is wiped
out by a virus unlike any seen before.

A mysterious visitor clad in a space suit checks his
handiwork, a female American doctor succumbs to the
disease, and the woman sent to trap the person
responsible falls in love with him – the man who would
cause the deaths of millions.

Hostage of Islam

Three are to die at the Mission in Nigeria: the pastor and
his wife in a blazing chapel; another gunned down while
trying to defend them from the Islamist fighters.

Kate McDonald, an American, grieving over her
boyfriend's death and Helen Campbell, whose life had
been troubled by drugs and prostitution, are taken by the
attackers.

Kate is sold to a slave trader who intends to sell her
virginity to an Arab Prince. Helen, to ensure their
survival, gives herself to the murderer of her friends.

Malika's Revenge

Malika, a drug-addicted prostitute, waits in a smugglers'
village for the next Afghan tribesman or Tajik gangster to
pay her price, a few scraps of heroin.

Yusup Baroyev, a drug lord, enjoys a lifestyle many would envy. An Afghan warlord sees the resurgence of the Taliban. A Russian white-collar criminal portrays himself as a good and honest citizen in Moscow.

All of them are linked to an audacious plan to increase the quantity of heroin shipped out of Afghanistan and into Russia and ultimately the West.

Some will succeed, some will die, some will be rescued from their plight and others will rue the day they became involved.

ABOUT THE AUTHOR

Phillip Strang was born in England in the late forties. He was an avid reader of science fiction in his teenage years: Isaac Asimov, Frank Herbert, the masters of the genre. Still an avid reader, the author now mainly reads thrillers.

In his early twenties, the author, with a degree in electronics engineering and a desire to see the world, left England for Sydney, Australia. Now, forty years later, he still resides in Australia, although many intervening years were spent in a myriad of countries, some calm and safe, others no more than war zones.

Made in the USA
Middletown, DE
23 August 2020